parABnormal Magazine

March 2024

Edited by H. David Blalock

parABnormal Magazine
March 2024

All rights reserved. No part of this book may be reproduced or transmitted in any form or by any means, electronic or mechanical, including photocopying or recording or by any information storage and retrieval systems, without expressed written consent of the authors and/or artists.

parABnormal Magazine is a work of fiction. Names, characters, places, and incidents are products of the authors' imaginations. Any resemblance to actual events or persons, living or dead, is entirely coincidental.

Story and illustration copyrights owned by the respective authors and artists.

Cover illustration "The Haunting" by Brian Quinn
Cover design by Laura Givens
First Printing, March 2024
Hiraeth Publishing
http://www.hiraethsffh.com/

Visit http://www.hiraethsffh.com/ for online science fiction, fantasy, horror, scifaiku, and more. Support the small, independent press...

Vol. VI, No. 1, Issue 21   March 2024

parABnormal Magazine is published quarterly on the 15th day of March, June, September, and December in the United States of America by Hiraeth Publishing, P.O. Box 1248, Tularosa, NM, 88352. Copyright 2024 by Hiraeth Publishing. All rights revert to authors and artists upon publication except as noted in selected individual contracts. Nothing may be reproduced in whole or in part without written permission from the authors and artists. Any similarity between places and persons mentioned in the fiction or semi-fiction and real places or persons living or dead is coincidental. Writers and artists guidelines are available online at www.hiraethsffh.com. Guidelines are also available upon request from Hiraeth Publishing, P.O. Box 1248, Tularosa, NM, 88352, if request is accompanied by a self-addressed ***10 envelope with a first-class US stamp. Editor: H David Blalock.

Contents

Stories
6	The Consolation for Piano by J. L. Royce
21	Flesh on the Mountains by Matthew McKiernan
39	Who Controls the Sea by LH Michael
50	Proof of Concept by Chris A. Bolton
65	The Committee by Emie Baines
75	Ongweias and the Stone Coats by Ken Leland
90	Last Confession of a Luftwaffe Ace by Douglas Kolacki

Poems
37	Kitsune by Chris Dickinson
38	Did You Say Something by Tom Guldin
49	Debris by Sarah Cannavo
89	Haunting by Mark A. Fisher

Articles
106	The Lazzaretto and the Ghost Child by Viviana de Cecco
112	Trilogy of Terror: The Horror of Female Archetypes Explained and Reversed by Denise Noe

A Little Help, Please

In the world of the small indie press we fight a never-ending battle for attention to our work, as writers and in publishing. Here's an example: big publishers [you know who they are] have gobs of $$$ that they can devote to advertising and marketing. Here at Hiraeth Publishing, our advertising budget consists of the deposits for whatever soda bottles and aluminum cans we can find alongside the highways. Anti-littering laws make our task even more difficult . . . J

That's where YOU come in. YOU are our best promoter. YOU are the one who can tell others about us. Just send 'em to our website, tell them about our store. That's all. Just that.

Of course, we don't mind if you talk us up. We're pretty good, you know. We have some award-winning and award-nominated writers and artists, plus other voices well-deserving to be heard [not everyone wins awards, right?] but our publications are read-worthy nevertheless.

That number once again is:

www.hiraethsffh.com

Friend us on Facebook at Hiraeth Publishing

Follow us on Twitter at @HiraethPublish1

What???

No subscription to parABnormal Magazine??

We can fix that . . .

Just go here and order:

https://www.hiraethsffh.com/product-page/parabnormal-magazine-subscription

...also makes a great gift any time of the year

The Consolation for Piano
J. L. Royce

Evelyn du Prinn sat with affected ease in her therapist's office. At his question, she forced out a sharp laugh.

"Oh, I'd never do *that*!" The pianist waved a slender arm. "What do you expect me to do, slit my wrists?" She leaned toward the therapist seated across from her. "And if I failed? I'd most likely damage the nerves, or what have you, and never play the piano again."

Owlish, her counselor studied her. "There was a previous attempt—"

"Accident," Evelyn said forcefully. She patted her hair, freshly coiffed by her stylist (though touched with gray she refused to recognize) and launched into the familiar explanation.

"I was drinking, admittedly, and confused my sleeping pills with my headache tablets. It's that simple."

He nodded, expression thoughtful. "Were you out with friends, drinking?"

Evelyn's lips were a thin line. "No."

He slowly composed a note, pondering her response, while she idly considered the drab familiarity of his shadowed office. Their 'conversation' was yet another performance.

"When you were younger—"

"Teenage angst. I was under so much pressure to excel at the piano, and my tutor..." She shook her head. "Well, if you don't have any other questions..."

"Are you seeing family during the holidays?" he asked.

"Family?" Evelyn shook her head. "Travel is so hectic this time of year."

"Perhaps you're planning to spend some time with friends here in town? Someone special?"

She stood abruptly and smoothed her skirt in a gesture her audiences around the world knew: *the performance is over.* "Music is my life."

The therapist smiled and carefully closed his notebook, rising. "Next week, then."

"Yes." She forced herself to return the smile. "I must be off—rehearsal this afternoon—but first there's a piano for sale on the Upper East Side."

"Do you need another piano?" he asked in his guileless manner.

"Of course not; but someone in the Symphony mentioned that it might be worth a look. And it will be a pleasant diversion."

Evelyn hurried to the elevator, her doctor trailing behind. "Expecting many friends at the concert tonight, since you're performing in town?"

"Friends?" Evelyn glanced down at him with a vague expression. "I suppose."

The elevator arrived, and she ducked past an exiting passenger to board it. As the doors closed she noticed the therapist reopening his notebook.

***

Other buildings in the trendy neighborhood had been renovated into multimillion-dollar condos, but this apartment was a sad dowager, untouched for nearly a century.

A young woman in a business suit answered the door and introduced herself as Heather.

"Ms. du Prinn, it's *truly* a privilege to make your acquaintance!"

Once-fashionable furniture was mostly enshrouded in drop cloths. "Where is your instrument?" Evelyn asked, taking in the gloomy surroundings.

"Oh, I'm an employee—"

"And the owner?"

The woman glanced into the dim depths of the apartment. "She's...unavailable. I'm an assistant to her attorney." She produced a business card that Evelyn dropped into her bag.

Heather beckoned to the pianist. "It's in here."

Evelyn slipped off her simple cloth coat, an affectation denying her wealth and privilege, and casually handed it to Heather in passing. Bemused, the assistant slung it over a covered chair and followed Evelyn into the front room.

The study was high-ceilinged, its built-in bookshelves empty save for discarded newspapers. The heavy drapes had been drawn back, the sunlight penetrating from the urban canyon beyond, and the air glowed with dust. On the far wall, a hearth stood massive and cold as a crypt. Evelyn wrinkled her nose at the stale medley of confinement and disuse.

The piano was a triangular shape longer than a coffin, carelessly covered in a filthy painter's drop cloth. Evelyn lifted the canvas and dragged it onto the floor with a moue of distaste, retreating as a cloud of dust rose.

It was a Steinway B, a semi-concert, just shy of seven feet long. Perhaps a half-century old, its deep maroon finish was clouded and grimy with neglect. Evelyn, always hunting the wayward Bechstein or Bösendorfer, was disappointed at the mundane *marque*.

A faint moan drifted in from somewhere down the hallway. Heather hurried to Evelyn's side.

"She's bedridden—nothing physical, apparently; the doctor says she could live to be a hundred! But some peculiar dementia, or so I'm told." The young woman shook her head—*the horrors of aging.* "I'd better see…"

"Yes, do that," Evelyn agreed, with a flash of distaste for the young and their attitudes toward their elders. "I'm fine here." Heather hurried off, and Evelyn turned to the instrument.

Despite her disappointment, Evelyn lifted the lid and propped it up, peering at the harp, the soundboard, the dampers, looking for the inevitable effects of the years. Though the interior smelled vaguely of mice she could see no droppings: perhaps recently vacuumed.

All in all, everything appeared to be in order. It was the sort of instrument that might serve a serious musician for a lifetime—a composer or teacher or performer like herself. Evelyn had examined many instruments, including counterfeits, and knew their value.

From her oversized purse, Evelyn drew a man's handkerchief. She snapped it open and spread the cloth over the bench, then sat and uncovered the keyboard.

It had been recently dusted, and Evelyn reluctantly

removed her gloves. Hands poised above the keys, it occurred to her that the moment was not unlike a first kiss, the prelude to intimacy, the promise of making something beautiful together. Smiling at such a girlish, romantic notion, she closed her eyes and smoothly ran scales up and down, finding nothing to criticize in the instrument's action. While considering a trial piece, another groan startled her.

She grimaced but launched into the etude, concentrating on the piano's voice and not the pitiful human distress beyond the room. When she finished the brief piece, Evelyn looked up to find Heather standing in the doorway.

"You play so beautifully!" the young woman effused.

"Chopin's beautiful. I'm merely his latest set of hands. Your client—is she alright?"

"Unfortunately, the sound of the piano agitates her—it's why we're selling, sadly—so if you're quite through..."

"You expect me to purchase an instrument I haven't evaluated?" Evelyn asked. "Who is *she*, anyway?" She tried to recall any recent departures from the concert scene.

"Our client prefers anonymity."

Evelyn rose. "I see. Well, perhaps when the owner is feeling well enough to make a personal appearance—"

A louder groan interrupted their exchange. Heather frowned and said, "Excuse me—please—stay as long as you wish." With that, the assistant hurried away.

Evelyn took up her handkerchief, shook it out, and folded it back into her bag. Ready to depart in disappointment, her gaze lingered on the bench. She idly lifted its lid, wondering what the contents might reveal about the owner.

The only piece of music was in manuscript ivory with age, though in good condition and free of dust. Evelyn lifted the half-dozen staff sheets and stared at the title, written in an elegant cursive hand:

La Consolazione per Pianoforte

Handwritten, there was no publisher nor a printing

date. The notation was quite precise, in ink that had aged into a deep umber.

"My consolation prize," she murmured and closed the bench lid. "Let's see what we have, shall we?"

Evelyn flipped up the music stand and arranged the sheets, skimming the piece, fascinated. There was no composer indicated, though the last page bore an intricate sigil. It took her a moment to recognize it as a pattern of four initials, entwined like vines: *AM & BB*.

Handkerchief forgotten, she sat before the keyboard and raised her hands.

"D Minor..." She inhaled, paused in a moment of uncharacteristic uncertainty, then shrugged it off and played.

Two themes circled each other like wary animals, like forbidden lovers. Ensnared in the music, Evelyn had reached the fourth page of the composition when a scream interrupted her enchantment.

"Christ!" At the sound of a clamor beyond she lurched to her feet, nearly upsetting the bench. Heart pounding, Evelyn glanced at the doorway, then back at the manuscript before her.

Perhaps it was the disappointment of the unexciting, albeit serviceable, instrument, or the irritation at the interruption, that triggered what happened next. Without hesitation, Evelyn gathered up the sheets, stacked them, and shoved the manuscript into her bag.

As she withdrew her hand, a pain as sharp as a cat's claw pierced her middle finger. With a hiss she stared at the blood oozing from a paper cut, dripping onto the sheets below.

"Damn!" She sucked her fingertip.

Heather appeared in the doorway. The assistant ran a hand over her disheveled auburn hair and said, "I'm sorry —I thought you had left."

Evelyn dropped her hand. "Just on my way." She pushed the bench beneath the keyboard with a foot. "I'll let you know what I decide."

With that, she strode past the assistant, grabbed her coat, and escaped with her prize.

***

The next morning, after the concert and the attendant rush of adulation, Evelyn rose refreshed and excited by the puzzle of the *Consolation*. As soon as she had dressed, she called her old mentor.

"Yes?" Ewan Stuart's voice came over the line.

"It's Evelyn," said the pianist.

A Baroque ensemble playing in the background immediately fell silent.

"Evie!" The pleasure in his voice poured over her. "Lovely performance last night."

"You were there?" she asked.

"I wouldn't have missed it. The reviews were glowing, dear! So—to what do I owe..." After a moment's hesitation, he said, "Ah; of course—your final piece. Unfamiliar..."

On impulse, Evelyn had added the *Consolation* as an encore, eliciting a second standing ovation from the delighted audience.

"I'm going to send you a photo," said Evelyn. She snapped a picture of the manuscript's first page and messaged it, then waited impatiently for his reaction.

"Did you get it?" she blurted. "What do you make of it?"

"Intriguing...From the style of the opening, we would surmise it's early Romantic."

"Do you recognize the style, the composer?"

"It's handwritten, with a very clean and confident approach. I don't know the hand, though there may be telltale personal quirks in the script. To distinguish whether it's period or copy work, I'll need to examine the manuscript itself—if that's alright with you."

"Of course."

"If I may ask, how did it come into your possession?"

Evelyn demurred. "I borrowed it from a friend. Do you recognize the opening?"

"It's new to me, and likely unknown to the public."

"There were initials...wait." Evelyn snapped a picture of the last page and transmitted it. "See?"

"Yes...four letters—composer and patron? Or...a dedication? I'll do some research."

"Thank you! I'll send photos of the other pages. And I should be able to bring the manuscript by, say, next week?"

"Yes. Meanwhile, I'll share anything I find."

***

"The concert—it was a wonderful evening!" Evelyn smiled.

The therapist nodded. "Your mood has improved since our last visit."

"It's as if the windows have been flung open." She glanced around the room, which felt different. The drapes were pulled back, suffusing the usually dull chamber with the soft light of a clear winter afternoon. "Are those fresh flowers?"

"So, you were pleased with your performance," he said.

"Well, it was more than that. I felt a genuine affection from the audience." Her hands embraced each other as she recalled the congratulations and the appreciation at the after-party.

She leaned back, legs crossed, foot bobbing.

"Has anything else happened?"

"Well, there is the new piece I performed as an encore. A bit of a mystery. And then there was a curious dream..."

She'd had it several nights, each time more detailed, more compelling. Her eyes wandered the room, searching the vertices, reassembling the impressions lost to wakefulness.

"I was playing the *Consolation*—my new piece—though not at home, or on stage. Someplace else. And I was younger. Someone was watching, standing behind me. Though I wanted to stop, to turn and look at them, I couldn't seem to."

"And how did you feel when you awakened?" the therapist asked.

"Oh—fine! Excited." She licked her lips. "I mean, energized. Wanting to go to the piano and play."

"Play the *Consolation*."

"Well, yes."

"Have you thought any more about the holidays?

Treating yourself, seeing friends?"

"Excuse me? As I said, no plans. Besides, my audience is full of friends."

"But that is a *transactional* relationship, yes? Don't you have anyone who cares for you as a person?"

Still alight with the pleasant memories of the concert, she was surprised to see the look of concern on his face.

"Your hands," he pointed, "are you in pain?"

"What?" Evelyn glanced down and realized she'd been wringing them. "No, they're a bit achy; perhaps I overexerted." She laughed and laid them to rest in her lap.

After their session, her counselor led Evelyn out to wait for the elevator. He reached out to touch her sleeve with a tentative gesture.

"Evelyn, I wondered if I might invite you to dinner. You seem to have no commitments for the holidays, and you're not traveling. Or sooner, if you permit..."

Evelyn blinked at him. "I don't know..."

"It's perfectly proper," he hastened to add. "We're not in the office." He laughed. "Or I could quit my practice!"

He grew serious. "I don't know why I couldn't see this earlier, what I've missed in life, and what a special person you are: talented, smart...attractive—"

The elevator chimed, and Evelyn fled into the small car. She rapidly punched the *Lobby* button.

"We'll talk!" she called, as the door slid shut.

***

In several emails, Professor Stuart had revealed the likely composer—one Aureliano Mezzasalma, born in Italy, trained in Paris, and living in New York City at the time of his death in the 1880s. The links the scholar provided, and the searches Evelyn performed, revealed him to be a controversial figure with a colorful personal life and a tragic death by his own hand.

Evelyn brought the manuscript to the Professor's Music Department office. Files and sheet music cabinets crowded the cramped space. He rose from behind his cluttered desk, the delight on his lined face apparent when Evelyn handed him the envelope.

"Ah, Evie! Let's see what we have here..."

Watching him draw on nitrile gloves, Evelyn was momentarily abashed at her casual handling of the manuscript. He spread the sheets across his desk, caressing them with bent fingers, murmuring to himself.

"Is it Mezzasalma? And who is *BB*?"

At last, he straightened and faced her.

"From the age, it *may* be his hand. Though we need to investigate the provenance of the manuscript." He stared at her.

"Of course," Evelyn said, thinking of the gloomy apartment and its distressed inhabitant. "I'll try."

Removing his gloves, he sat down and slid a grimy keyboard out from beneath his desk. An ancient CRT screen came to glowing life. At her bemused expression, the Professor remarked, "So? It still works."

Evelyn squinted at the grainy image of a tall, bearded man with deep-set eyes and dark, unruly hair.

"That is *AM...*," Stuart explained, "and we may surmise that this is *BB*, the love of his life, his obsession, his downfall..."

The screen flickered and Evelyn stared at multiple photographs of a woman, youthful yet somehow sly and experienced. The earliest showed a girl in a long dress with pale waves curling to her shoulders; the latest, an elegantly dressed and coiffed ingenue. Evelyn idly wondered about the couple and the mystery of infatuation, its genesis and course.

"Blisse Brisbois, as musically talented as she was beautiful," the Professor went on. "She was Mezzasalma's student in Paris until her parents learned he sought to make her his lover as well. They dismissed him, but he fled to the United States, New York, taking her along. She was sixteen."

Evelyn straightened. "What became of them?"

"Public opinion held Blisse blameless in the affair, but society ostracized Aureliano. He wanted to marry her, despite the wife he had abandoned in France. Instead, with a promising career ahead of her, she found a rich society patron and abandoned her teacher."

He shook his head. "It was his ruination. He blamed

everyone but himself—her parents, New York society, and eventually Blisse. Poverty no doubt contributed to his ill health, as did his laudanum addiction. He likely took his own life with an overdose."

He fell silent, staring at the manuscript pages.

"Was there anything more to their story?" Evelyn asked.

The Professor blinked. "Ah, just foolishness. He confronted Blisse at her society coming out, chiding her for flaunting her beauty rather than perfecting her art. As he was ejected from the affair, Mezzasalma threatened she would 'forever remember her betrayal with regret'."

"And did Blisse achieve success?"

He shrugged. "Her career peaked early. Perhaps she was too enamored of balls and suitors. Blisse was barely in her twenties when she had a breakdown and disappeared from public view."

"Can you access a catalog of his compositions?"

"Indeed." He tapped away at the keyboard and a list appeared on the screen. "Piano works—several dedicated to Blisse—altogether a small collection. Some real talent, as you heard in the *Consolation*. Which makes this—" he tapped the pages "—priceless."

Professor Stuart nodded to himself. "I'd like to make a copy, just as insurance."

Evelyn nodded. "Of course."

She watched him carefully scan the pages on a flatbed multifunction copier, then return them to the envelope. Finally,

he sank into his chair and crossed his hands on his paunch with a sigh, gazing up at her. "Your performance was beautiful...just like you," he said.

Evelyn laughed it off. "Now you're being silly."

"I have a confession to make. When you were my student, I was perhaps as smitten with you as Aureliano was with Blisse. But I lacked the courage to pursue you..."

"Professor—"

"Ewan—can you call me Ewan?"

"Ewan, I've always cherished our friendship. Thank you for all your support over the years."

"And now you're successful, and attractive, and I'm... old."

Evelyn placed a tentative hand on the man's shoulder, leaning over to retrieve the envelope.

"Please let me know what you learn," she said. "Perhaps we can have coffee together and discuss it?"

He brightened and smiled. "I'd like that."

"Good. I look forward to it!" She hurried towards the door.

"And Evie..."

"Yes?"

"I noticed you're rubbing your hands. Do take care not to overexert yourself in your practice."

"It's nothing," she replied casually. "It will pass."

***

In that quiet hour of the Manhattan night, after the bars had closed and before the garbage trucks had arrived, Evelyn dreamed again.

Again, she was at the piano. The music she played, the *Consolation*, flowed through her, arousing her all the more, now that she knew its story. She knew it was a man standing behind her, and that he felt it too. The hands floating effortlessly across the keyboard were unblemished, a youth's, and her hair drifted loosely about her face, longer than she had worn it since college.

Evelyn could feel him close to her, knew he was naked, and sensed his arousal. She wanted more than anything to rise and embrace him, pleasure him, but even as the thought formed, he spoke a single word.

Play.

Evelyn shuddered and awoke. Her gown was damp, and her hands, clamped between her thighs, were hot. She withdrew them and stared at the reddened digits. As she watched, they trembled. She threw back the covers and strode off to the shower.

At her vanity, hair wrapped in a towel, her gaze went from her face to her hands and back again, wondering at the changes. Even sans makeup, her cheeks glowed with health, and her neck was firm and smooth. Evelyn knew her hair, when dry, would shine with the sable luster of her youth. Reluctantly she turned her attention to her hands, applying a steroid cream to the raw skin, the digits aching with a deeper irritation, in the joints, the tendons: her instrument.

She dressed, chose a pair of gloves, and slipped them on, hissing at the pain. Even so, her hands longed for the keyboard. But a car awaited her for the drive back to the source of the *Consolation*.

***

Arriving unannounced, a young Latina in midnight blue scrub pants and top answered the door.

"I'm a friend." Evelyn smiled broadly and stepped past the surprised aide. Heather was not there to meet her—or restrain her.

"How's she feeling today?" she asked, and strode back into the apartment without awaiting a reply.

"The patient is sleeping," said the aide. "Shouldn't be disturbed."

"Oh, she'll want to see *me!*" She glanced in passing at the shrouded piano and other deserted areas before arriving at a door ajar near the back of the flat.

Someone had attempted to lend the room a cheery air. Light poured through the bright, sheer drapes, and the bed was made with gaily flowered sheets and counterpane, the latter turned back in the warm sunlight. The occupant lay supine, propped up on pillows, her eyes closed.

The woman looked barely old enough for the title. Golden hair spilled across the pillows, framing an attractive face. The sheet could not disguise her graceful frame. Evelyn studied her, convinced they had met but unable to recall how or when. The sleeper stirred, legs restless.

Her confidence faded. Evelyn reluctantly crossed the room, eyes drawn to the woman's hands, encased in bulky, fingerless mittens, curled like a boxer's into fists. Recognition snapped into focus, and she murmured, "Olivia Raenard…"

The lids flew open, long lashes fluttering before amethyst eyes.

Evelyn started.

"I didn't mean to disturb you—"

"Olivia..." repeated the woman.

"Yes—you heard me—a friend from school." Evelyn laughed. "Of course, that was years ago."

They had fallen out of touch when Evelyn went to Europe on her breakout tour: two pianists struggling to establish themselves, one successful, and one...

"Evelyn..." The blonde struggled to rise.

"Why, yes!" her visitor replied, assuming her fame had preceded her. "Are you related to Olivia?"

The patient tried to push herself upright with bent wrists. As she considered Evelyn, her full lips curved into a sardonic smile.

"*You* played it!" She tossed back her blonde waves and laughed.

"I, ah..." Evelyn stammered an explanation. "I came about the piano and found a manuscript in the bench. Where did it come from, by the way? Why do you have it?"

"The *Consolation*...I had a position in piano pedagogy at Columbia, though I also performed—in small venues, nothing like *your* success. I was researching the American contributions to the Romantic movement and came across the manuscript misfiled in the University archives. I included it in my repertoire."

She sighed. "I lied, said it was my composition; I stole it—though not the way you did." Her head cocked to one side as she stared up at Evelyn. "What a twist of Fate; after all these years..."

A memory stirred, awakened by the familiar story, and an uncomfortable, impossible suspicion teased Evelyn.

The woman eyed Evelyn's gloved fingers, even now dancing lightly on her thighs in an involuntary rhythm. She struggled to rise against the pillows.

The aide lingering in the doorway stepped in and hurried to her patient's side. "Ms. Raenard, let me help."

"How—more drugs? To keep me sedated?"

"You are related to Olivia, then?" pressed Evelyn.

The woman laughed again, a bitter bark. "I *am* Olivia."

The suspicion affirmed, Evelyn stood speechless as the aide eased her into a sitting position.

"Take these off!" demanded Olivia, waving her swaddled hands.

"It isn't time for your treatment—"

"Take off these damn mittens! Let her see!" Leaning forward, Olivia thrust the bulbous white appendages at the aide, who glanced back at Evelyn, dread in her dark eyes, then bent to the task.

Reason struggled to suppress Evelyn's shock. "But you're my age," she said, watching the mittens loosen with rising apprehension. She glanced down at her own gloved hands.

Olivia nodded. "Do you think these covers are to protect my hands? The experts were useless—they thought if I didn't play, then—" she winced and glared at the woman tugging at the gauze beneath "—then my condition would 'stabilize'."

"Aureliano Mezzasalma," said Evelyn.

"He poured himself into that piece—his blood and soul, his anger and lust—to punish his beloved Blisse. His curse: she could have the beauty she craved, but she could only have her music as long as she played his *Consolation*."

Evelyn realized that her hands ached not in pain but in desperate need of the keyboard, that she longed to rush out to the Steinway in the library and pour out his notes, to channel his passion.

"They chose for me, the fool doctors—they took away my music, said this was all in my mind." The last of the wrappings fell aside and the aide turned away. Olivia raised her arms, and Evelyn gasped.

The hands looked ancient, the emaciated digits curled into writhen claws, tendons shortened as though by the fires of Hell.

"See how pretty you can be?" Olivia murmured, turning them slowly. Tears gleamed in her crystal eyes as she ran a misshapen finger down her soft cheek. "When I stole his work, I forfeited my chance. Perhaps you'll find a balance between beauty and art—if Mezzasalma achieves his fame, through you."

"What shall I do?" Evelyn whispered.

"Play," said the blonde, lowering her hands with a grimace. "Play the *Consolation* as though your life depended upon it."

"And you?" Evelyn asked.

"The music is yours now," Olivia Raenard replied. "Go."

Evelyn stumbled towards the door, but paused to glance back.

Olivia was turned to the window, perfect skin awash in the soft light, hair gleaming golden.

"I shall make a lovely corpse."

Flesh on the Mountains
Matthew McKiernan

January 26, 1864

    This isn't my journal, but given the state of its owner, I see no harm in commandeering it. After all, these may be the last words I write. I'm Corporal Elijah Anderson of the Union Army. I enlisted after the bombardment of Fort Sumter and survived The Battle of Gettysburg. I guess the best place to begin all this would be yesterday afternoon. We were bunkered down at the base of the mountains. It had been snowing nonstop for almost a whole week. Our food supply was scarce, so Sergeant Levi Weston, the son of a fur trapper and the most formidable man I knew, was ordered by Lieutenant Gates to go hunting.

    He took me along with privates Simeon Donnovan and Wiley Lemsky. The only hunting experience I've had was some squirrel hunting at my uncle's ranch. When I told Levi this, he said it was better than nothing, which was all that Wiley and Simeon had. It had stopped snowing at dawn, but I could tell by the sky that it could come down again at any moment. I prayed the snow wouldn't return till evening. I didn't want it to cover all the tracks, even though Levi said there were other ways to pursue an animal.

    Levi was someone who always caught his own food for the campfire. He said eating anything in a tin can will weaken you. Levi never drank a drop of alcohol. I drank whenever I had the chance to make the nightmares go away, but it never really worked. I don't know if Levi didn't drink because he was half-Indian or because he might have been one of those Mormons. His father had four wives. According to Levi, his mom was his dad's favorite. Besides that, he didn't talk much about his life back home. He always told me that if you focus too much on what's waiting for you when you get back, you'll lose what you have here.

    We set out to hunt deer, but, before we knew it, we

were tracking a moose. Now moose may be related to deer, but according to Levi, they were more aggressive than grizzly bears and a lot stronger too. While deer run, moose attack. We'd have one shot to bring the beast down, or it would destroy us with its hoofs.

Well, I hadn't come this far to be killed by a dang moose. Levi crouched beside some bushes with a few strands of fur on them. He yanked it off and sniffed. "Looks like we're not the only ones after that moose. Some wolves are giving us competition."

I gripped my rifle. While Simeon became frozen in place, Wiley shuffled around. His beady eyes whirled about as though he expected wolves to come at us at any moment. "Oh God, wolves...we should go... back to... camp right now," he stuttered.

Simeon nodded through chattering teeth. I didn't want to get between wolves and their meal either. At the same time, though, I didn't want Levi to think I was a coward. Levi brushed some snow off his shoulder. "Wolves aren't as scary as your momma's bedtime stories. They normally don't bother people unless you wander into their territory or own livestock. The truth is, they are more afraid of us than we are of them."

All I knew about wolves was from fairy tales like *Little Red Riding Hood* or others with less pleasant endings. From Levi, though, I learned that wolves don't hunt alone. They hunt in packs. One wolf was probably less dangerous than a moose, and probably way easier to kill as well. However, a whole pack wasn't something I wanted to encounter. So, I said, "Be that as it may, I don't think we should get between them and their prey. Let's go hunt something else."

Levi stood up. "There's nothing else around. But this isn't such a bad deal. If we play our cards right, the wolves can do all our work for us."

I couldn't believe what I was hearing. "You want the wolves to kill the moose and then have us take its carcass from them!"

"That's complete madness!" yelled Wiley

"Yeah, that will put us in their bellies!" Simeon added.

Levi shook his head. "No, it can be done. We just need some fire!"

There were pine and larix trees all around us, but Levi said they weren't good enough. He made us search around till we found a mahogany tree. Wiley, Simeon, and I climbed up and used our bayonets to sever four of its branches, but Levi used a hatchet that he always carried with him. He also carried a red satchel that contained rope and other useful items. When we finally cut the branches and took off the twigs, Levi pulled out a piece of flint. He eyed the large copper whiskey flask that Wiley always kept around his hip. "Hand that over."

Wiley did so. "What? Are you going to start drinking now?"

"Hardly. There are so many better uses for alcohol."

He poured the whiskey atop the branches and pulled out a piece of flint. It took a few tries, but he managed to get all four branches lit. I don't think they would have lightened up the night, but they passed as torches. We each took one, as Levi explained, "Wolves hate fire. Whenever they see it, they flee as far as they can. So, we need to track them down, wait till they make their kill, and then rush at them as though hell is behind us."

"I don't know about this," Simeon said, "How do you know for sure they'll be more afraid of us than losing their meal?"

Levi chuckled. "You'd know all about that, fat boy!"

Simeon's face went red like the inside of a watermelon. "Maybe I'm guilty of gluttony, but at least I'm not a damn half-breed!"

Levi went for his hatchet. Wiley and I got between them. We managed to calm Levi down but didn't get him or Simeon to apologize. I like to think it was just hunger that had everyone on edge, and the fact that we were about to take on wolves. Levi was running beside their tracks with the rest of us struggling to keep up. I guess he was in his element since this is what his life had been like before the war.

Wiley had been a lawyer and often still acted like one. Simeon had done nothing till he'd been drafted. He just dwelled at his mother's house, fattening himself up. I'd known him for a month, and for whatever odd reason, he never lost any weight. Fencing lessons and working at my uncle's ranch managed to keep me in shape and prepared me to be a soldier. Still, I wasn't cut out for all this wilderness stuff like Levi was. I'm too attached to the trappings of civilization to ever want to be free of it.

The four of us moved along, following the snow prints. Even though I'm no tracker, I could tell the wolves were running neck and neck with the moose. With every step I took, I felt this was more and more a dumb idea. Then again, I had survived headlong charge after charge into rebel gunfire during the war. I told myself that this couldn't be more dangerous than that. Eventually, the trail of tracks turned into one of blood that led to a small hill.

The moose was at the bottom of the slope, lifeless. It or I guess I should say he since he had the most enormous antlers and testicles I have ever seen. Yeah, I'll say he. He was lying on his side, with bites all over him. His throat had been shredded open, and the moose's belly had been gnawed at. The wolves were nowhere to be seen.

Levi slid down the hill. I was happy to stay on top of it but decided to follow him. I stumbled when I was halfway down and barely managed to avoid falling on my rifle. Levi dashed over to the moose's corpse. He traced his fingers over the beast's wounds. "Six wolves took this big boy down. Guess they had some advantage since it's blind."

I looked at the moose's eyes. They were whiter than the snow. Imagine going through life surrounded by endless darkness! Maybe a moose wouldn't mind, but that would make me go mad. Although perhaps I'm going mad already. Levi examined the footprints encircling the moose. "This doesn't make any sense."

"What doesn't make any sense?"

Levi darted about as he exclaimed. "The wolves killed the moose, and just when they were starting to dig in, something spooked them away."

"Maybe they heard or smelled us coming."

Levi squatted and tapped his knuckles against the

paw prints. "No, no, that's not it. There was something here that came upon the wolves after their kill."

"A grizzly bear?"

Levi shook his head. "They're all hibernating now. Loud noises could indeed wake them up, but they're not able to eat. Besides, even you would notice if a bear had been here."

"You're right. There's nothing but the wolves' tracks."

I looked at Simeon and Wiley, who had stayed on top of that hill. I suddenly wished that I had stayed there too. I think the cold was finally starting to get to me because I felt a shiver run down my spine. Oh, who am I kidding? That was pure fear. "Well, we got our moose. Let's hack off what we can and return to camp."

Levi got up. "No, we need to find out what's chasing after those wolves. Because like any predator, it will come back for its prize, and I need to know what we're dealing with."

Levi dashed off, and I yelled for Simeon and Wiley to come down. I did not want to chase after something that terrified wolves. However, I wasn't going to let Levi wander off on his own even though I knew it would probably get us all killed. Also, I didn't want to leave the moose behind for scavengers.

As we followed Levi, a strong wind blew out our makeshift torches, but Levi kept going. It wasn't long until we arrived at the wolves' den. The den was a burrow in the ground, surrounded by jagged gray stones protracting from the earth like spikes. The bodies of nine wolves were scattered all around those stones. Six adults and three weren't exactly puppies, but they weren't fully grown yet either. All the wolves had gray fur except the white one. I knew by his size that he must have been the pack's leader. He died after being hurled against one of the jagged rocks and having the back of his skull burst apart. Three wolves' necks were sliced down to the bone. One's entrails were spilled open. Another's head had been squashed. A female gray wolf, who I like to think was the white wolf's mate since she was as big as he was, her heart had been ripped out. The smallest of the wolves had been torn in half.

The last wolf had mange. I could tell because of the bald patches along his fur. This wolf had died from having all his legs snapped off like some insect. Simeon nudged some of the dead wolves with his rifle. Wiley shouted a crescendo of curses that I shall not record here. Levi looked pale and more afraid than I'd ever seen him before. Then again, I don't think I've ever seen him scared. These poor wolves didn't deserve to be killed like this. Nothing does. I could tell that whatever did this, hadn't even tried to eat them. I wouldn't even say that it killed for sport. It massacred them for nothing. I wondered if it was still around. What chance did we have if it could slaughter a whole wolf pack?

After Wiley finished ranting, I asked. "What in Christ's holy name could have done this?"

Levi blinked several times before answering. "Nothing, there is no animal I know of that can kill an entire wolf pack."

Wiley said nothing, but I'm sure his mind, all our minds, were drifting to the idea that a creature of the natural world hadn't done this. I wondered which of us would be the first to say the word monster. Simeon wiped the spittle from his mouth. "We should hightail it out of here before whatever or whoever did this, decides to return."

"Let's get back to the moose," I said.

Levi shook his head. "Let's not waste any time backtracking and cutting the moose up. Instead, we'll hogtie one of the wolves and take it back with us."

We used one of the torches to tie the white wolf's feet around and ditched the others. Wiley and Simeon carried it while Levi and I walked beside them, weapons at the ready. Now I wanted us all to run back to camp, but Levi said that would make us all sweat, and sweating in the snow is one of the fastest ways to freeze to death. However, I recall that sweat was already trickling down my neck.

Levi found a path where the trees became sparser until they were gone. The four of us were armed with Springfield Rifles. In the hands of a good soldier, they could shoot three rounds a minute at a distance of five hundred yards. Whatever killed those wolves would be fully exposed if it came at us. Although if we missed, I don't know if we'd get a second chance at another shot. My deepest fear was that there might have been more of them who killed the wolves. Since it, or they, didn't leave tracks, it was impossible to know its number. Snowflakes the size of blueberries descended. I should have been happy that the clouds held back as long as they did, but I would have preferred it if they had held back until we returned to camp. A strong gust scattered surface snow all around us.

We were surrounded by white. If anything came at us, we wouldn't see it until it was in striking distance. If the weather got worse, we might not be able to see anything at all. I shivered so severely that my rifle started to shake. I tightened my grip and decided I should say something to brighten the mood. "So, Levi, do you have an Indian name?"

"Why are you asking me that now?"

"I don't know. I guess now just feels like the time to ask."

Levi sighed. "Red Crow. I'm probably the only Indian. Well, half Indian to ever climb up these mountains."

"Why is that?" I asked.

Levi told me of the dreadful monster the Indians of this land feared. I wondered if that was the fiend that did the wolves in, so it wouldn't have any competition for human meat. I put those thoughts aside. The gale started to lighten up. Enough so that I spotted three figures approaching us through the snowfall, about a dozen feet away. Like us, they were covered head to toe in snow, but I could still make out the color of their uniforms. "Graybacks!" I hollered.

A shot rang out, blowing my kepi off as I slammed to the ground and returned fire. I shot off the cap and upper left ear of the man who shot at me. A bullet grazed Levi's right arm. He kept standing as he fired his rifle and hit nothing. Wiley and Simeon dropped the wolf and whipped out their guns. They fired. None of the confederates had fallen. The one in the middle pulled a handkerchief from his coat. "Truce! Truce! Truce!"

I had my finger on the trigger, but it went still at that word. I looked at Levi. As the highest-ranking officer here, he would have to head out. Levi took a deep breath and set aside his rifle and hatchet. He checked his arm out. It didn't seem to be bleeding much. Levi marched over to the Confederates; hands held high. I should mention that two of the Graybacks were armed with Enfield Rifles. The one with the handkerchief, who had blond hair, didn't have a rifle. Instead, he had two holstered Colt revolvers around his waist and a saber strapped to his back. He was a cavalry rider with no horse. The blond southerner made his way to Levi but didn't extend the same courtesy of discarding his weapons. They met in the middle and talked. I couldn't hear them over the wind. The rebel whose upper ear I had shot off was squatting, trying to hold his gun while covering his wound. The other confederate had lowered his rifle.

I put some distance between my trigger and my finger, so I wouldn't be the one to end up doing something stupid. Levi and the blond-haired confederate chatted for five minutes or so. They shook hands and returned to their respective sides. Levi rubbed his wound and said, "All right, we talked things out. None of us are returning to our camps in this weather, so the Confederate and I decided to find a cave to spend the night, share the wolf and go our separate ways when morning arrives. The storm should be over by then."

I felt like I'd been punched in the gut. "You want us to break bread with those sons of rapists!"

Simeon protested. "I agree with the corporal. This isn't a promising idea."

"We should write down all the terms of the truce in a legally binding document," Wiley needlessly interjected.

Levi put his weapons back on. "Listen, I'm not thrilled about this either. But right now, we got to put everything else aside and focus on surviving through the night."

"I'd rather freeze to death or die by whatever did those wolves in," I hissed.

Levi grabbed me by the collar. "I know how you feel about slavery and the South, Corporal Anderson, but you're under my command and will obey my orders. Is that understood?"

I have never disobeyed an order before, even the ones I hated. This though, how could I do this? I have been killing these traitors for three years now. Was I just supposed to forget all that for the evening? Forget about the friends of mine they killed or who lost limbs and had to go home as less than full men? Should I forget about the millions of poor souls they have in bondage? Or that this war was their damn fault?

Still, it's not like the Graybacks hated us any less. They could have fought us for the wolf's carcass; instead, they called a truce. A truce must be honored. I had never killed anyone outside the battlefield, and there was no need to start doing that now. Besides, the longer we stayed out and argued amongst ourselves, the more likely the wolves' killer would find us. "When we get back, I'll tell Lieutenant Gates I opposed this."

"I can live with that," Levi replied. "Now, let's go greet our southern brothers."

We all shook hands and introduced ourselves. The confederate whose upper ear I had shot off was Ensign Harmon Roundtree. Ensign Aaron Sappington was the rebel who looked like he wanted to be anywhere but here and gave me the most halfhearted handshake of my life. He also had the yellowest teeth I have ever seen. The blond cavalry officer was Captain Felix Ammon.

He asked if we had any cigars and was disappointed to hear that none of us smoked. We all exchanged jokes and pleasantries like we were at some gentlemen's club. Harmon even offered to help me find my hat. However, it was now buried in the snow with his hat and the piece of his left ear. It was decided to have Aaron and Simeon carry the wolf carcass together as an act of compromise. While they hoisted it up, Felix stuck a finger into the wolf's skull cavity and stirred it around. "By golly, how did you Yankees manage to kill a wolf like that?"

I was going to tell the blond traitor that wasn't his

business, but Levi cut me off. "I'll tell you about it while we search for shelter."

I was about to protest, but I realized there was no harm in Levi telling them our hunting tale. When Levi was done, the rebels laughed. "You expect my men and I to believe that something killed a whole wolf pack and didn't leave one trace behind? Not even a footprint?" Felix quibbled.

Levi replied. "It's the truth; I'll give directions to their den so you can see it yourselves."

Felix snorted. "Yeah, we will not be doing that."

I wanted to call Felix a coward but held my tongue. The wind picked up again. Soon it became a full-on blizzard. I couldn't see my hand, even if I held it in front of my face. There was no warmth left in my body, and so much snow ended up in my boots, that my feet were numb. Levi ordered us to grab each other's shoulders and march in a line.

I don't know how, but we must have ended up extremely high on a mountain to the point where breathing took tremendous effort. I wanted to take off my coat and all my undershirts just to relieve the pressure on my chest. I was still coherent enough to know that would be my death. This would have been so much better if we had a lantern. Just having one shred of light and warmth would have been enough for me. "I think I spot a cave up ahead!" Levi shouted.

I had no idea how he could see anything at this point. Felix shouted back. "One of us should scout ahead. To make sure it's unoccupied."

"That ain't going to be me!" Harmon hollered.

It wasn't going to be me either. Before I could say anything, something pushed Harmon, knocking us all down like a stack of dominoes. I scrambled back up as screams echoed all around me. I couldn't see anything. I was blindly waving my rifle, deciding where I should fire. "It took the wolf. It took the wolf!" Simeon screamed.

"What?" I yelled

A hand reached through the wind and grabbed my rifle. It was Felix. I had to stop myself from firing. "Grab onto me."

I did so, and together we rounded everyone else up and managed to make it to the cave. I let myself collapse on its snow-free floor. I gave my eyes a good rubbing until my vision cleared. There were only six of us. Levi was gone. "Where's Levi?"

Nobody answered. So, I screamed out. "Levi..."

Felix knelt and covered my mouth. "Shut up! You don't want it to hear you!"

I must have been in terrible shape. Even though his hand wasn't pressing on me that hard, I blacked out. I woke up nestled against the cave wall. Wiley was by my side. We had moved deeper into the cave while I was unconscious. The entrance was nowhere in sight. That's why nobody saw any harm in starting a fire. They used some cloth scraps, shoelaces, and Felix's giant hat. Speaking of Felix, I didn't see him anywhere. I figured out correctly that he was guarding the opening to the cave. Although a cavern this big, most likely had another entrance, I thought Levi would know where to look for one. Then I remembered that he was gone. I sprang up and uttered. "What happened? Did anyone see what attacked us? Where the hell is Levi?"

Everyone's faces had a disheartening look that I knew only too well. Wiley coughed. "He's dead, Elijah. Whatever attacked us killed him."

"Tell me how he died!" I demanded.

Felix appeared. He'd turned the stick we had been carrying the wolf with back into a torch with a soft glow that lit up the cave. He had blood splattered across the upper half of his uniform and it wasn't his. "It took your sergeant's head clean off. I guess your story about the wolves was true, after all."

I got up. "You were behind Levi, so you saw it, right?"

Felix toyed with his blond curls. "I don't know what I saw. It was just a blur. One second your sergeant's head was on his shoulders. The next, it wasn't."

"Did anyone else see what happened?" I asked.

Everyone was silent. Felix's men couldn't even say anything. Something had assaulted us. Of that, there was no doubt. Still, how did I know this rebel hadn't killed Levi in all the confusion? That wasn't the most rational thought, but I can't say I was in a sensible state of mind. "Show me your saber!"

"You don't have to listen to him, sir!" Aaron shouted.

"That bluecoat's out of his mind if he thinks you could do something like that," Harmon added.

Felix ignored them and drew his saber. In the light of the torch, I could tell there wasn't a speck of blood on it. Never in my entire life had I felt like such a fool. "I'm sorry, he was my friend."

Felix said nothing. He just sheathed his blade and went back to exploring the cave. Wiley finally got the fire going. I sat between him and Simeon, who handed me Levi's hatchet. "I scooped it up. I think he'd want you to have it."

I stuffed the hatchet into my belt. After losing so many friends to battle and sickness, I thought this wouldn't bother me as much. But it did. There is no getting over losing those you care about. I don't know how I would explain this to Lieutenant Gates. I also wondered if I should write to Levi's family, then I recalled that none of them knew how to read.

Felix returned and dropped a human skull and leg bones by the fire. Wiley gasped. Simeon looked sick, and the two rebels crossed themselves. "It looks like we're not this cave's first occupants. Aaron, you've warmed up enough; stand guard at the entrance."

"Go with him, Wiley," I ordered.

Wiley gulped from his flask and left it for us. Felix gave Aaron his torch and sat down. Harmon had some hardtack which we divided up and washed down with Wiley's whiskey. After having my fill, I handed the bottle to Simeon. I gazed at the bones. In the flickering of the fire, I could see marks on them, the kind that can only be made with a knife. Felix noticed them too and picked the skull up. He twisted it around. "Looks like this poor man was a victim of cannibalism."

"How do you know it's a man?" said Simeon.

"Do any of us want it to be a woman?" Felix snapped.

I've seen men butchering each other for years. But a woman, no, I can't think of the gentler sex being harmed like that. But still, cannibalism! That's the kind of thing you make jokes about the enemy doing. But to see a real example of it sickens your soul. "Do you think Indians did this?" inquired Harmon.

I responded. "There are tribes that practice cannibalism. But those in this part of the country feel the same way about it that we Christian folk do. Besides, no Indian would set foot on these mountains anyway. Levi told me they believe...."

My hands were shaking even though I wasn't cold. I dreaded saying the words I was about to speak, but I somehow managed to. "They believe that if you eat human flesh on the mountains, you become a *Wendigo*. A horrendous monster that survives only by cannibalism since it can't consume anything else."

Simeon began scratching his fat belly, which he often did whenever he was nervous. "It's just a superstition. Like leprechauns."

Felix unsheathed his saber and tapped the tip against the ground. "Why don't we change the subject and talk about the number of men we've killed?"

"Do you think that's a good idea?" I questioned.

Felix responded. "It's better than where you're leading us. How about you go first, Corporal Anderson?"

I tightened my hands into fists as my fear faded and was replaced by fury. "Eleven, I've killed eleven of you, traitors!"

"Ah, three..." mumbled Simeon.

"I've put fourteen of you union boys in the grave," Harmon grinned.

"I've killed fifty-seven men." Felix bragged.

I slapped my knee. "That's a bunch of hogwash. I don't care how good you are. There is no way you've killed fifty-seven of us!"

Felix prodded the flames with his blade. "I didn't say I killed fifty-seven of you northerners. I said I killed fifty-seven men. You see, while you and your friends were out hunting game, we were hunting deserters, because that's what I do. I track down those cravens and kill them on sight. I've killed far more "traitors" than you."

Felix burst into a fit of snickering, and Harmon joined him. But I didn't think anything about that was funny. I wiped away some sweat that was forming on my brow. "I agree that deserters deserve to be executed, but they should also be tried before a military tribunal. Doesn't the Confederacy still give men that right?"

"We have far fewer men than you do and far more desertions. So certain rights had to be sacrificed." Felix replied.

It didn't matter what side of a war a man was on. To be hunted down and killed like an animal wasn't right. "Well, maybe you wouldn't have so much desertion if you were fighting for a worthy cause."

Felix stopped poking at the fire. He gripped the hilt of his saber and looked me in the eye. "I think my cause is very worthy."

"Why, so your slaves can work themselves to death at your plantation?"

Once those words left my lips, I worried I had gone too far. If Felix attacked, would I be able to bury my hatchet into his neck before his saber got me? Felix ran a hand over his face as his scowl turned into a smile. "My family runs a schoolhouse. I've never seen a plantation or a slave. I fight for my country. Tell me what origins you hail from?"

Putting my foot in my mouth hadn't ended up being that severe a blunder. Still, I felt embarrassed to speak of my background. I rubbed the back of my head as I explained. "My father owns a shipping yard and several other businesses. Also, my mother is a Belgian countess."

Felix and Harmon burst into a fit of chuckling once more. This time Simeon joined them. When it ended, Felix tapped me on the shoulder, and I held back my urge to break his arm. "Boy, you're, Mr. Humble."

I could feel myself blushing. "Fortune has been good to my family, but we give back. My parents have donated all kinds of money to the fight against slavery. I wanted to do something more, though."

Simeon drank the rest of the whisky and burped. "For the record, I want everyone here to know that I don't give a damn about slavery one way or another."

He turned to look at me and continued. "I'm sorry, Elijah, but you abolitionists always make things more difficult."

I struck Simeon in a place no man wants to be hit. That earned another round of laughter from the rebels as Simeon moaned and rolled around like a grub. A screech echoed through the cave, making my blood run cold. The worst part was, that it wasn't coming from the entrance. It was coming from the back of the cave. I helped Simeon up. Felix sheathed his blade and pulled out his revolvers. We formed a line and aimed our guns at the dark. "Aaron, Wiley, get over here!" I shouted.

Aaron and Wiley rushed over and joined us. The screeching got louder and louder. However, we all held firm and kept our hands on our weapons. The shrieking ceased. A figure emerged from the darkness. It had to be a Wendigo! Oh God, it was so much worse than the story Levi had told me! Its body was emaciated. It was just bones with skin hanging on them. The creature was naked but didn't have any genitalia.

Its fingers were long and sharp as an eagle's talons. There were two sunken black holes where the monster's eyes should have been. The monster's wide mouth was filled with dozens of needle-like teeth. Its long tongue was blue and wiggling like a worm. Only a few strands of brown hair atop its head showed it had ever been human. We fired, although Aaron and Harmon's guns didn't go off. The snow must've dampened the powder in them. The Wendigo lurched back as our bullets made impact. I was thrilled to see that abomination bleed. It charged at us, knocking Felix down.

It disemboweled Simeon and bit off Aaron's face. I tried to stab it with my bayonet, but the Wendigo yanked the rifle from my grasp and broke it. I still have no idea how something with no muscle on it could be so strong. Harmon tried what I attempted. It plunged his rifle through him. I sliced at the Wendigo with my hatchet, cutting its left shoulder. The beast screamed and swiped its claws at me. I pivoted back, slipped, and fell on my bottom. Harmon chucked his rifle aside and tried to tackle the monster from behind. It flipped him over and stomped its foot on Harmon's neck, crushing his windpipe. Wiley managed to get another shot off. The bullet went into the back of its skull, but it still lived. The Wendigo turned, grappled Wiley's arms, and ripped them off.

Felix got up with blood seeping from his forehead. He peppered the Wendigo with bullets, causing it to back away from me. I sprang up, raced to Felix, and pulled his saber from its sheath. I lunged at the fiend, hacking at it with my hatchet and saber. With my blades and Felix's bullets, we overwhelmed it. The sound of gunfire ceased. Felix had run out of ammunition. He gave a rebel yell and bashed the grips of his revolvers against its head.

It slashed its claws at us and slit Felix's neck open. I barely dodged them and got my face gashed. I hurled the hatchet, embedding it in the Wendigo's chest. With both hands, I swung my saber at its head. I sliced off everything above the monster's jaw. It disintegrated into dust. I dropped the blade and dashed over to Felix. I put my hands on his throat and tried to apply pressure. But there was so much blood. I couldn't do anything.

Felix's vocal cords must have been severed because he couldn't make a sound. He grasped my wrists and managed to crack a smile. I grinned back. "I'm proud to have fought beside you, Captain Ammon. Blue or gray, you are the bravest man I've met."

Felix nodded as his eyes closed. He was gone. Everyone was gone. It was just me. I shed tears for all of them, even the rebels. Then again, when we fought against that disciple of Satan, we weren't Union or Confederate soldiers. We were just men trying to survive. I took my hands off Felix's neck. I saw a tear in his upper uniform. A black leather book poked out. It was Felix's journal. I didn't read his entries since they aren't my business. Instead, I skipped to the blank pages and decided to write down all that happened today. The storm is still raging outside, so I can't leave this cave anytime soon.

The Wendigo's gash runs from my right eyebrow to my chin. It's been bleeding on and off, but I think it's finally stopped. As I stated previously, these might be the last words I ever write. The wind is carrying another unholy screech that has been going on for three hours. It's getting closer and closer. This time though, it sounds like there's more than one of them.

Kitsune
Chris Dickinson

"Come here my love, my dear, dear one—come here
Unto the rushes by the river's side;
And there will we in love's embrace abide,
And offer one to other endless cheer.

Do not behind me look—there's nothing there...
Why do you now a lover's plea deride?
For you alone my lips do open wide.
This kiss...a promise of how you may fare."

So saying, did the beauty lead the man,
And by the stream let fall her silken robe
On which they laid as on a downy bed.
A fox's eyes her lover's face did scan
And nine soft fox-tails did his form enrobe.
She left—and in her hand her lover's head.

Did You Say Something?
Tom Guldin

voices in the dark
soft whispering and echos,
past habitation —
    wife nudges me to wake up
    "Did you say something?" she asks

Terminal
H David Blalock

Quiet sits behind the dawn
Silent as the dying night
Hushed as voices stilled in death
Soundless as footsteps forgotten

Now calm, peace rules
Where life roared, deafening
Now shut are throats
That, open, cried despair

The end consumes all pain
In quietude eternal

Who Controls the Sea
LH Michael

Instead of shaking Lee's hand, Martina handed him a coffee.

"Uh, thank you?" Lee said.

Lee and his daughter were at their church that Monday for a Thanksgiving food drive. He didn't recognize Martina, and hadn't requested the coffee, which swirled in the sort of Styrofoam cup that comes with an ozone hole.

"They always make too much," Martina explained.

Though he had his eyes on the exit, Lee sensed that declining the coffee would drag out his departure.

"Nice to have a coffee for the road on these cold days. Hi, I'm Lee."

"I'm Martina. Is this your daughter?" she said, pointing to the 8-year-old holding Lee's hand.

"Yes, this is Isabelle. Isabelle, say hello."

She said it.

Martina quizzed Isabelle, "What does your shirt say?"

"Sloop-of-War. It's a ship."

"We visited the Harbor last summer. My daughter loves ships," Lee said.

"Me too. Well, how about that."

"Let's go, Isabelle. Nice meeting you," Lee said.

When they stepped outside, Lee dumped the coffee in the first trash can he saw.

***

14 days later, while volunteering at the church, Lee and his daughter crisscrossed with Martina again.

"How about some coffee?" was still her opening line.

"I'm good. Thanks."

"Glad I bumped into you. I'm going to give you something."

"Really, if it's coffee, I'd rather you gave it to someone else."

Martina's bottom lip skewed.

"You don't even know what it is," she said.

She disappeared behind the basement door and emerged with her right arm behind her back.

"Ready?"

Martina handed a doll to Isabelle and said, "Merry Christmas!"

"I am not sure we can accept this," Lee commented.

"I made the doll myself. She likes ships, that's what you told me."

The crudely-hewn doll exemplified the Captain Bligh style, right down to its buckled shoes.

"I was going to give her a ship in a bottle, but what fun are those?"

"What can I say? Thank you very much. Isabelle, what do you say?"

"Thank you!"

Pam Allegria, a university student who also shouldered volunteer work at the church, came near. Lee blocked her path and said, "Pam and I here, we have a lot to do. Thanks again, Martina."

"Thank you!" Isabelle said. She extended her hand. Martina shook hands with the doll.

***

"What do you know about that woman?" Lee asked Pam once they'd taken their places in the office.

"Who? You're talking about Martina? What about her?"

"What does she do here?"

"She's in charge of the AA meetings or whatever it's called."

"AA meaning Alcoholics Anonymous?"

"Yup, Mondays, they all meet down in the basement. She organizes or something."

I never would have gone to this church if I'd known they hosted AA, Lee thought.

"How long have they had meetings at the church?"

"Only a month, probably."

Isabelle, who should have been stuffing envelopes, rotated the doll in her hands.

There was a squeak outside the door. Martina dipped her head in the office.

"Everything all right in here?" she said.

"All good," Lee said.

"Be careful driving home, everyone. Rainy night out there. Nothing the captain of a ship can't handle," she said, looking at Isabelle.

***

The doll, whom Isabelle named Jack Tar, had curly, auburn hair that looked human, and a flowing jacket that featured many pockets. One contained a teabag, a small pipe reposed in another. Lee couldn't unsee the disparity between the doll's exquisite clothing and its chunky, misshapen body.

Isabelle's favorite toy ship, the *Normaund*, boasted the perfect dimensions for Jack Tar. When he stood on its bow, it was as if he existed to captain that vessel alone.

***

"Isabelle? You left your barrels all over the stairs. I almost stepped on them."

The tiny wooden barrels came with a ship purchased for Isabelle by her uncle.

"Jack Tar put them there."

"No, he didn't. Now clean this all up."

"Jack Tar won't let me have them in my room."

"Really? And why won't he?"

"He says they're full of rum."

***

Isabelle stepped to the front of the class.

"Are you ready?" her teacher, Ms. Moritz, asked.

"Ready! My story is named 'Driving Home from O'Grady's'. Marty said it was time to go. We all drank what was in front of us. When I got outside, I couldn't find my car. Then I saw it between two trucks. I think I banged my door against one of the trucks. My door definitely ended up with a scratch on it. I ran over a trash can when I drove out of the parking lot. I don't remember how long I was driving, but next thing I remember, I was stopping in the driveway. I was so drunk I don't remember how I got the front door open, but I went into the living room and found a bottle of liquor. The glasses weren't where I usually put them. I opened the bottle and took a few gulps. Vodka, I think. I never drank vodka. I heard someone come downstairs. I expected to see Margaret, but the woman who leaned over the stairwell screamed, 'Get out! Get out!' I was in the wrong house. I ran for the door. I got to my car, but couldn't find my keys. I checked every pocket. I saw they were in the ignition. I drove around the corner so fast I hit a curb. I don't even remember getting home, but I woke up in my own bed. The end."

"Isabelle? Where did you get this story?" her teacher gasped.

***

"Isabelle? Where did you get this story?" her father yelled.

"It wasn't me!"

"So, who was it then? Where'd it come from?"

She shrugged.

"What have I told you about lying! When you do something bad, first thing you must do is tell the truth about it. The truth."

"Ms. Moritz told everyone we had to write a story for the class. I sat down on my bed with my notebook, but I don't remember after that."

"Hold on, what is that smell in here? It's like coffee or something."

On the carpet, next to the *Normaund,* four dolls cloistered in a circle. Two held mugs.

***

Oh no, here comes Martina, Lee thought. Need to leave the church before she sees me.

"Lee!"

Too late.

"Hey there, Martina.

"Happy Sunday. Are you here with your daughter?"

"She is with her grandfather."

"Where is her mother?"

The question rumbled him. His ex-wife Robyn wasn't a subject he volleyed with people he barely knew.

"Her mother is not in the picture."

"You're divorced, then?"

"Something like that. You're coming from your alcoholics' meeting?"

Lee hadn't intended to mention AA, but it came out. It

was rude. It felt great.

"No, today, I am here for my first mass."

"It's your higher power step?"

Her face contorted as a dog's does before vomiting.

"How is your daughter liking the doll I made?"

"She plays with him."

"What name did she give him?"

"Don't know," Lee said, not understanding why he'd fibbed.

"I would have thought she'd tell you the name."

"Who knows why she didn't tell me. The doll you made doesn't really fit with her other dolls, I have to say."

"It's not supposed to fit with the others," Martina said with Atacama dryness.

"Right, I know, handmade."

"That isn't what I meant."

"What did you mean?"

"He cannot ever be like the others. He is their *leader*."

***

Lee squeezed the steering wheel as if wadding it into a spitball. *Why did Martina focus so much on Isabelle? And to just come out and mention divorce? Why did AA always spell bad news for him?* His ex-wife Robyn, spent plenteous time at AA meetings. The candor the program fostered alienated her from everyone not acquainted with Bill W, until finally, she ran off with her sponsor.

Lee slammed his car door, then slammed the front door of his house. He grabbed a crystal tumbler. He'd never gone much for booze, and seeing how it sank Robyn hadn't sweetened its appeal. Still, he'd received a bottle of 100 proof vodka from his boss, and 100 proof vodka has a place in this world.

He popped open the liquor cabinet and nearly dropped his tumbler. Wrapped around his vodka bottle was Jack Tar.

Lee moved his hand towards the vodka. It tumbled out. He caught it, but the doll's body went flying. One of its plastic hands remained stuck to the bottle.

His phone rang. Unknown caller.

"Hello?"

"Do you hear me, Lee?"
"I'm sorry, who is speaking?"
"This is Martina. How is Jack doing?"
"How'd you get my number?"
"We go to the same church. How is Jack doing?"
"I don't understand what you mean. Who is Jack?"
"Jack Tar."
The doll, he thought.
"I'm not following you, Martina. I have to say, your calling me is not appropriate."
"You have deeper problems at the moment."
"What is that supposed to mean?"
"I saw it in you the very first time we met."
"What did you see?"
She didn't answer.
"Okay, listen, don't ever call me again. All right? Just stay out of my business."
"When you stop living in the problem and start living in the answer, the problem goes away."
She hung up.
Lee realized he'd never told her Jack Tar's name.

***

He propped the tumbler on top of the liquor cabinet and poured. The doll's still-attached hand tweaked him. He couldn't understand why Isabelle had appended her doll to the bottle.

The tumbler reached his bottom lip. His phone buzzed. He didn't recognize the number. It went to voicemail.

It rang again. Same number. Voicemail.

It rang again. He gave in.

"Hello?"

"Oh, thank God. I'm so happy I could reach you. I want to see you, is that all right? We need to talk, so many things we need to discuss."

He was afraid to say the word, "Robyn?"

"Of course, yeah, it's me. Who else? I was getting worried when you didn't answer right away."

"What is it you're calling about?" Lee asked.

"I want to see you. I am staying nearby."

"What is it you want to discuss so much?"

"Lee, I can't. Truly, I can't. Not right now, at least. Not like this, on the phone. Let's have lunch tomorrow. Can we do that? You can meet for lunch, can't you? I'm pretty sure you can."

"You sure we can't clear whatever it is we need to clear up right now on the phone?"

"We haven't seen each other in forever, Lee. I've done what I told you I would do. I haven't contacted you, even though I guess I probably should have."

When he needed them most, his nerves went on shore leave. He agreed to meet her the next day for lunch. He hung up and returned to his vodka. The doll hand floated in his tumbler.

***

He circled Isabelle's room, wanting to source the coffee odor. He knocked against her nightside table, which knocked a notebook onto the floor. There were scribblings across the visible pages. The handwriting resembled Isabelle's, but looked older somehow. He peeked over his shoulder twice before reading.

The first page said, *I'm Matthew, and I'm an alcoholic. When I got out of rehab the first time, it had been a year since I'd had any sort of proper job. I had no money. I broke into my grandmother's house when she wasn't home and took her jewelry.*

Lee turned to another page.

My son was in the backseat when I crashed the car.

Lee examined another page. There were coordinates etched in the corner, like one finds on a ship log. *Marty said it was time to go. We all drank what was in front of us. When I got outside, I couldn't find my car.*

It was the story Isabelle had read in class.

Lee flipped to a passage with almost calligraphic writing.

We were at a pool at the house of a friend of ours. I don't remember how many glasses of wine I drank. Five or six. My sister tried doing a flip off the diving board and hit her head. She went in the water and didn't come back up. I jumped in the water but I was so drunk I couldn't swim towards the bottom. My sister never came to the surface. She drowned because of me.

Lee scanned to the top of the passage. It began, *I'm Martina and I'm an alcoholic.*

***

Robyn had stocked herself in a booth near the diner's eastern window. She looked ragged, though no worse than when he'd last seen her.

"This is really weird. Don't you find this weird?" she said when he came near.

She went through the menu item by item, reading the descriptions out loud.

"How is Evan?" Lee asked, hoping a question about her second husband might shock her into congruity.

"Did you say Evan?"

"I did. How is he?"

"He's not around really anymore."

"Does that mean the two of you are no longer together?"

In between dead calm pauses, Robyn shared her news about Evan, the AA sponsor with whom she ran off:

Evan had vanished a month earlier. He'd gone out sailing with his friend Yidong. When they didn't return, the authorities went looking. Authorities located the boat (which was in perfect condition), as well as Yidong's body. They couldn't smoke out of a trace of Evan.

Lee interrupted to ask, "Is this why you're drinking again?"

"Why did you say that? What makes you think I could be drinking?"

"I smell it."

She sat up extra straight. "It's not every day, okay? I don't drink every day. Sometimes, when I drink, all I do is sip. I've only really done real drinking a couple times since he left."

"So what, a month then?"

"More like two months."

"You told me he'd been missing for a month."

"Before that, okay, he'd moved in with this other woman. Don't laugh at this, but he left me for a girl who was his sponsor. His sponsor! Martina was her name."

His abs twinged.

"What did you say her name was?"

"Martina. That's her name."

"And he met her in AA?"

"That's what I just said. You sound like you might be drunk!"

Lee received a text from his father, "Bringing Isabelle home," it read.

"You know what's funny? Well, not funny, bizarre. There's a woman, at our church, her name is Martina."

"And what? There can be more than one Martina in the world. Trust me. Last few weeks, I've been hunting lots of Martinas. Now listen, we're way off the topic now!"

He logged onto the church's website and screened the event calendar.

"Robyn, I need to go."

"You're going? Now? No. Lee, no, wait, we only just got here. I don't know when I'm going to see you again."

Hopefully never, he thought.

***

Lee slunk through the church door and found Martina posted near the holy water fountain. She wore elf clothes.

The lobby had kids and adults packed in every corner. Soda, candy, and boisterous voices abounded. Every year, the church held a gift drive for kids in need. He'd never seen it so well attended. Three children, accompanied by adults, waited online for presents.

He felt around in his right coat pocket and joined the line. He didn't know yet how close he should get.

Behind Martina sat a life-sized Santa doll. Its red and white hat hung crookedly over its face.

He crouched to prevent her from seeing him. The line advanced.

The kid conversing with Martina was too shy to say much. The line advanced. Only one kid (and her mother) stood between Lee and Martina.

He used his phone to zoom in on the Santa doll's face. Its curly, auburn hair looked identical to the hair on Jack Tar.

Martina spotted him. She smirked and said, "If you're here to make amends, you're too late."

"Martina!" a woman yelled.

Lee knew the voice. *Robyn followed me here*, he thought.

Martina's face paled. She dipped her hand in the holy water and mouthed two words to Lee, "Too late."

Robyn kicked through the Christmas display, rolling over the Santa doll. Its outfit came open. Its chest had a doll shape carved into it.

She chased Martina through the pews. The crowd followed, ordering her to stop.

Lee threw the Santa doll over his shoulder and rushed out of the church.

***

Lee heard panting as he entered the house.

"Dad? Isabelle. It's me."

The panting came from the second level. He climbed the stairs, increasing his speed while pretending not to.

"Isabelle? Hello?"

His father lay in front of the bathroom, battling for breath.

The bathroom door was open. Isabelle lay face down in the filled bathtub. Jack Tar sat on the faucet, holding a harpoon.

Lee retrieved his daughter from the water.

"Isabelle!"

He commenced CPR, wishing he could hand over all the breath in his body.

"Breathe!"

He pressed. He stretched his lungs. Something bumped his foot. His father.

"What happened here?" Lee screamed.

His father coughed and jerked along the ground like a perishing mackerel. The thought of swapping his father's life for his daughter's corseted Lee's mind.

Isabelle coughed. Lee's father stopped coughing. Jack Tar plunged into the water.

***

The doctors iterated to Lee, in terms both layman and

scientific, that he'd been extraordinarily fortunate. He'd found Isabelle at the precise moment she'd stopped breathing. She'd be okay.

His father died at the hospital. Heart attack, they said.

Martina and Robyn were both missing. Both had escaped the church before police arrived. Lee was willing to bet at least one of them had ended up in a nearby body of water.

He walked across the backyard, carrying Jack Tar in one hand and dragging the Santa doll with the other. He lay the Santa doll flat and held its curly hair against Jack Tar's. Definitely the same. He pushed Jack into the cavity in the Santa's doll's chest. It fit perfectly.

He poured the 100-proof vodka all over the doll. Its eyes were moist and shining. Had the vodka splashed on them? He planted Isabelle's notebook on the doll's chest and tore out a page.

He wasn't positive, but the doll's cheeks appeared rosier. *Is it the vodka,* Lee thought. He placed the notebook page over the doll's face. The page moved almost imperceptibly, as if the doll exhaled.

Lee lit a match and said, "God, grant me the serenity to accept the things I cannot change, courage to change the things I can, and wisdom to know the difference."

He ignited the paper and waited to hear if the doll would scream.

Debris
Sarah Cannavo

> After the world ends
> only the ghosts remain,
> mournfully drifting through
> the rubble in search of
> homes that no longer exist.

Proof Of Concept
Chris A. Bolton

"Quit being a butthead, Jerry!" Claire snapped, bringing the entire room to a dead silence.

It wasn't the first time Claire had called him that this week. But now Jerry was trying to direct a roomful of pre-teens, which was a colossal ass-ache without having his kid sister snap at him in front of the whole crew.

"If you can't follow simple directions, Claire," Jerry shot back, "then go home. I'll reshoot your scenes with someone who can do the job."

Claire stared at Jerry with wide, wounded eyes for a few breaths, then glanced around as if she'd become increasingly aware that the cast and crew were watching her. Red-cheeked, she spun on one heel and stormed out.

Jerry considered whether he should go after Claire and talk her back. Reshooting her scenes would be next to impossible. As annoyed as he was by her increasingly defiant attitude, he felt sorry for embarrassing her in front of her friends and a bunch of strange grown-ups.

On the other hand, the crew worked twice as fast after she left. Her little friends stopped making fart noises and ran their lines like he'd told them to. Sometimes you have to kick a dog to keep the rest of the pack in line.

Turning toward the window where Eduardo's friends were installing the breakaway glass, Jerry caught a reflection of a silhouette—too dark to make out any details, but it seemed to be standing behind him.

When he glanced back, nothing was there but the stucco wall of the empty room. Apart from the cast and crew of *Grave Diggers*, the unfinished house seemed unoccupied. Jerry turned back to the window. Whatever he'd thought he saw was there no longer. His skin chilled and the knot in his stomach pulled even tighter.

God, he thought for the millionth time that week, *this movie had better work.*

***

"Claire, wait!"

She stopped at the foot of the stairs and looked at the

second-floor landing, expecting to see Jerry hurrying after her with an armful of apologies. Instead, Malachi hustled down the steps to her.

"You aren't quitting, are you?" he asked. "Don't leave me alone with Jerry."

"You'll be fine," Claire hissed. "You're the big star."

Malachi shook his head. "I don't know what I'm doing and Jerry hates everything I do. You should've been the lead all along."

Claire didn't disagree, but it was satisfying to hear him say it. No matter how hard she pleaded her case, however, she couldn't convince Jerry to recast her as the hero.

Malachi dropped his voice to a whisper. "I don't want to do the stunt, Claire. I'm..." He hesitated, swallowing loudly. "I'm scared."

Claire forgot her rage and saw her best friend since third grade really struggling: hands wringing, eyes goggling, sweat beading his forehead. "It's gonna be okay. Jerry won't let you do anything that could really hurt you."

"You mean, like, jump through a window?"

Claire opened her mouth, then realized she didn't feel like helping Jerry out. "You're right—I should do it."

Malachi reacted like she'd slapped him. "I wasn't saying that—"

"But I am."

It made sense: she'd been jumping off playgrounds since she could walk, taking risks that terrified her parents but impressed her cool older brother enough to nickname her "Danger Claire." That had been part of her disappointment at being cast as the girl who screams and cries and runs away from demonic spirits attacking her friends. How had she toppled so far in Jerry's eyes, from Danger Claire to helpless damsel?

"Play along like you're gonna do the stunt," she said. "When Jerry's outside and the cameras are rolling, I'll get on the bike and do it instead. He can only afford to shoot it once—so, he'll *have* to recast me as the lead."

Malachi had that look he got whenever Claire's face lit

up with a scheming grin. "Y'know, maybe I'm not as scared as I thought..."

But Danger Claire was sick of standing in the corner, half-ignored while she helped her ungrateful brother make his dream project a reality. She seized his hand and dragged Malachi up the stairs.

***

Jerry watched Eduardo's crew hammer the wooden ramp into place underneath the window. He was grateful for their help but couldn't shake the feeling they were laughing behind his back. He couldn't wait to cut the film together and show everyone how wrong they'd been about him.

He wished he could give one of them to the Presence. But it had been very explicit about what it wanted. He had no choice at this point: the sacrifice was demanded and would be given.

Eduardo popped in the doorway. "Ready to look?"

Jerry followed Eduardo downstairs through the empty house, trying not to think about how much was at stake in one shot.

He'd already dropped out of USC Film School. None of the goofy videos he'd shot with the family's Sony VHS camcorder had prepared him for the ruthlessness of the film industry. Those videos were celebrated among family and friends, but failed to impress his professors, fellow film students, or Hollywood professionals.

Jerry had crawled home to parents whose averted gazes revealed their disappointment. His once-fawning kid sister no longer seemed impressed by him. After a few weeks of nursing his sorrows, he read an interview with Sam Raimi, who talked about financing *Evil Dead* by shooting a proof-of-concept short that he showed to private investors, mostly dentists. Jerry's dad was a dentist who knew lots of other well-off dentists.

Jerry hatched a new plan: make a short film that he could use to raise the money for his debut feature. The idea came soon after: a group of young teens find a map that leads them to an abandoned house, where they battle a ghost guarding a treasure. A high-concept mix of

Goonies and *Evil Dead*, he called it *Grave Diggers*—and felt sure it would launch his Hollywood career.

As Eduardo led him out the front door, Jerry marveled again at his strange luck. His family had moved into this housing development just before the financing company went bankrupt and shut down all construction. Entire cul-de-sacs of homes sat untouched in various states of semi-completion. No one paid any attention to what Jerry did in one of countless empty houses with a small film crew and a barely adolescent cast.

Jerry had been just as lucky that his high school friend and perennial Director of Photography, Eduardo, was eager to shoot the film. He even brought along a gang of oddball refugees from community college film classes. Despite only being ten minutes long, the proof-of-concept for *Grave Diggers* was the most ambitious film project any of them had worked on.

They should have been grateful. But most of the time, he had the feeling they each thought they were better qualified to direct than Jerry. Even Eduardo, who'd been his enthusiastic collaborator on half those VHS shorts, seemed like he couldn't wait to shove Jerry out of the way and seize the throne.

But Jerry had made arrangements. *Grave Diggers* was his and no one—living or otherwise—would take it from him.

Jerry realized Eduardo was staring expectantly. "Well?"

He peered through the viewfinder at the shot. Another benefit of Eduardo's community college connections was the ability to check out the school's 16mm cameras, audio equipment, and lighting rig. It was simpler to shoot on VHS, of course—especially since it recorded sound in-camera and no volunteer ever wanted to hold the boom mic—but this would look and sound more professional. Easier for small-town dentists to imagine the movie their money would bring to life.

Jerry studied the angle carefully. This was the make-or-break money shot that, if it worked, would make checkbooks soar into the hands of eager investors—and, if it failed, would slam every door in Jerry's face. It had to be *perfect*.

"Almost," Jerry said. "Needs to be moodier. *Noir*-ish. It should feel like the house is alive. Angry. Doesn't *want* them to escape."

Eduardo gave him an unmistakable look: *How in God's name do I light a house like that?* But all he said was, "Okay, back at it."

As Jerry walked back across the lawn, Eduardo barked commands and the grips raced to move C-stands and bounce cards for the lights.

Jerry tilted his head back to take in the house, holding his hands in front of his face to mimic a movie screen. Although the house had never been inhabited, it gave off an ominous feel like something horrible had happened long ago and its dark echo resonated within the brown wooden slats. He knew it was a tall order, but he wanted that uneasy feeling to ooze from the screen and hit the viewer in the gut. Otherwise, it was just a cool-looking stunt that almost anyone could have put together.

Jerry froze at the front door. Inside the second-floor window on his left, the crew tested the makeshift ramp to be sure it would hold their weight.

On the opposite side of the house, a dark silhouette filled the right-hand window. The master bedroom was being used as a staging area to store backpacks, suitcases, and unused equipment. But all the crew members were in Jerry's sight and none of the kid actors were tall enough to fill the entire window.

Jerry shuddered as he tore his gaze from the figure. He felt its eyes on him every step of the way into the house.

***

Claire walked on set and was met with a flurry of annoyed voices from bored, aggravated eighth graders. They'd been stuck at the house since eight in the morning, wasting a perfectly good summer day at the end of a week in which they'd learned making movies was far less exciting than it looked on *Entertainment Tonight*.

"Why do we still have to be here?" Viet Nguyen

moaned. "We already did our scene this morning."

"That was the reaction shot," Claire said.

They'd been grouped in front of the window and told to imagine watching Malachi race past them on his bike, then crashing through the glass. Jerry had hoped to get their astonished reactions in one, quick take, but he didn't stop shooting take after take until noon.

"I'm bored," Misty Wilson whined. "I want to go home."

"You can't," Claire said. "We just need one more shot! Don't you want to be in a real, actual movie?" She turned to Viet. "You said you'd give anything to be one of those guys in *Goonies*. Here's your chance!"

Misty rolled her eyes. "Yeah, right. We'll be lucky if this thing plays on cable access."

Claire gnashed her teeth, wanting to scream at Misty that she was an ungrateful, untalented brat who didn't deserve to be in this awesome movie. She hadn't even *wanted* her in the shoot, but Jerry had insisted they needed one more girl in the cast. (Claire suspected Jerry was more interested in Misty's super-rich parents, who owned half the town.)

She was surprised to realize how protective she felt of Jerry and his film. In spite of all her frustrations, she still wanted him to succeed and would do anything to help him.

"Claire's right," said Lydia, the Assistant Director. "You can all go home in an hour—two, tops."

The kids grumbled amongst each other, not believing a word of it. When their attention drifted away from Claire, Malachi tugged on her sleeve. "For the record, I think this is a stupid idea. And I hate it."

"Well, for the record, I don't care," Claire said. "You don't want to get on the bike and I do. It's better for both of us."

"How's it better if you get killed instead of me?"

"It's not even *that* dangerous. And anyway, I've been practicing."

"You have?" Malachi asked, his dark eyebrows knitting together.

"Just a bit," Claire said with a shrug. "Jerry didn't

notice. Or care."

As much as she tried to cover it up, his disinterest had crushed her. When their front lawn was dug up to repair the shoddy septic system, Claire set up a wooden plank to launch her bike over the pit. She'd cleared the fifteen-foot gap with a bumpy landing on the sidewalk that ended in a triumphant sideways skid into the driveway.

But Jerry had only flung a perfunctory thumbs-up over his shoulder as he hurried past. Claire felt like a five-year-old in a pool, yelling at Jerry to watch how she can dunk her head underwater.

"If you break your neck..." Malachi looked terrified, which touched Claire. He certainly cared more about her than her older brother, at least these days.

"Don't worry," she said, patting his arm. "I'm Danger Claire, remember? Nothing ever hurts me."

Except Jerry, she thought bitterly.

She'd been jubilant for him to come home from college, eager to joke around and laugh at cheesy movies like they'd done her entire life. Instead, he either hid in his room with the door shut, moped around the house in sullen silence, or took long drives by himself. He never laughed and hardly acknowledged her existence.

When, after several weeks, he announced he was going to shoot a film, Claire practically crowed with joy. Every summer since she was six, she'd acted in Jerry's videos. Even though he was always the writer-director, she viewed them as *their* films—the fruits of an equal partnership that reflected their easy chemistry.

As had happened every time before—even when Eduardo started working with them in Jerry's freshman year and the movies changed from slapstick comedies to Hitchcockian thrillers—Claire expected to be the star. She and Jerry would regain their rapport and it would be another great summer having fun every day with her awesome brother.

But it didn't turn out that way. Even though she'd won Best Actor at her eighth-grade graduation—a ceremony Jerry had missed, to Claire's heartbreak—he wanted a boy as the lead for *Grave Diggers*. "It's not a *girl's* film," he'd said, which made Claire want to punch his sneering mouth.

He still needed Claire—to recruit all her friends from Drama class as the other actors. She'd half-hoped that rounding up the best of the best (and, alas, Misty) would put her back in Jerry's good graces.

And she knew she could out-act the rest of them. She only had one line, but she practiced it to perfection, preparing to erupt past her cast-mates with their stilted awkwardness in front of the camera. On the morning of her big scene, Jerry cut her line. "Just give me a reaction," he'd said—and the reaction she gave him was her middle finger, ruining an otherwise solid take and putting her squarely on Jerry's shit list.

They'd been at each other's throats ever since. Claire hated Jerry, but she hated hating him even more. This time, there was no line to cut. When he called "Action" and Claire careened through the fake glass, she knew Jerry would be enraged. But he'd get over that and realize Claire should be the star of his movie—and should have been all along.

She glanced toward the doorway, thinking she saw Jerry hurry past in that quick-but-quiet hustle that meant he didn't want to be seen. But when she stepped into the hallway and looked around, he was nowhere to be found.

***

Jerry crept up the stairs to the attic, moving as swiftly as he dared without attracting unwanted attention. He'd told the crew the attic was off-limits, claiming the floor was unfinished and they could fall through the ceiling.

In truth, the attic was as finished as it needed to be. Jerry ducked under the low, angled ceiling, crouching on bare boards and looking at sheets of exposed drywall, waiting to see the real reason he kept everyone out.

For his short film, Jerry had chosen to shoot the scene where the trapped kids try to escape from the ghost. Eduardo had suggested going the *Jaws* route, hiding the monster until the final reel to build suspense and save on effects. But Jerry was adamant they had to show the ghost, or nobody would invest.

The problem was, he had no money for decent visual effects. And he loathed the idea of putting an extra in a rubbery skeleton costume with cheesy makeup.

A solution presented itself unexpectedly. Jerry had picked the most decrepit house in the most isolated cul-de-sac to shoot in, and came back for inspiration during preproduction. He'd sketched a ghost concept that looked distinctive and unnerving: a black cloud with slender arms and a demonic face that looked carved out of charcoal.

Jerry wasn't sure *why* he kept coming back to the house every night, sketching the ghastly figure over and over, until the Presence revealed itself to him. He'd been sitting cross-legged on the attic floor, scribbling on the back of script pages, when he looked up to see the hideous face leer at him from a dark corner. The sight froze a breath midway up his throat and turned his skin to ice.

But when the Presence appeared in front of him now, Jerry felt only a mild prickle of his arm-hairs. "You aren't supposed to come downstairs," Jerry said. "If someone sees you..."

The Presence hovered above him, its flickering black shape reminding Jerry of the sketch-people in the music video for a-ha's "Take On Me." He sensed its agitation—or was it just impatient for its promised meal?

"You'll be able to take your... prize today." Jerry swallowed, unwilling to use the words *victim* or *sacrifice*. "In an hour or two, he'll be all yours."

To do what? Jerry shuddered at the very notion of what the thing had planned for poor Malachi. But that had been the price—not only for shooting at the house it occupied, but for its appearance on-camera. Jerry wouldn't need money for special effects—he was going to have a real, honest-to-God *ghost* in his film.

(Or demon. Or whatever it was. He was nowhere near certain.)

The Presence hissed at him. It never spoke, but a thought would enter Jerry's head, as clear as if the ghost had whispered it straight into his skull.

The thought he "heard" was, *I've waited long enough. I crave a fresh soul now.*

Jerry felt his cheeks flush. "You can't have it! You'll fucking ruin everything."

The Presence lunged at him. Jerry scrambled back, bumping his head against the decline of the roof. He caught himself on a wooden beam before he sprawled across the floorboards.

The Presence opened its skeletal maw a few inches from Jerry's gaping mouth. Its teeth were long, sharp knives carved from onyx. It reeked like an extinguished campfire, scorching his nostrils.

"Please," he whispered, realizing—too late—he wasn't the director of anything. Merely a servant of darkness.

The thought sprang into his head that he only continued living because the Presence permitted it. Because it wanted a *young* soul to feed on, filled with adolescent energy and brightness, all the more delicious when spiced with mortal terror.

But it could, with the smallest effort, extinguish Jerry like fingers on a match head.

"We have to get this shot," Jerry said. "Then you'll have him, like I promised."

The thought of the Presence feeding on his lead actor made his stomach queasy. Jerry tried to ignore it.

The footage would be utterly spectacular: Malachi on the bicycle bursting through a second-story window, hurtling toward the ground until a spectral figure swept down, snatched him in mid-air, and consumed his soul— *right on camera.*

And in an unbroken wide shot that couldn't have been faked.

A few times, sweating and fretting through a sleepless night, Jerry worried it would backfire. That the short film would become so notorious, nobody would give him a penny to make the feature. And it wasn't as if he could duplicate the shot for the feature-length version—nor could he use the actor who'd died while filming the short.

He always assured himself that the fame of capturing a real ghost on film far outweighed any moral qualms he had.

"Just wait a few another hour," Jerry said, backing away from the Presence, "until I get my money shot. Then you'll get everything you want."

Younger souls are juicier, a chilling thought warned him, *but yours is young enough to suffice.*

Jerry hurried down the stairs, not wanting to dwell on that notion a second longer. "Don't forget—the one you devour is the kid on the bike. None of the others. Like we agreed."

Jerry opened the door, peeked into the hallway to be sure it was clear, then stepped out.

As he closed the door behind him, Lydia stepped into the doorway of the staging room. "Eduardo's all set. And we're burning daylight."

Jerry smirked at her. "Magic hour, baby."

***

Walking out with tremors of excitement and anxiety, Jerry noticed the tower of gym mats topped by an upside-down inflatable pool packed with pillows. It was far from the airbags used by professional stunt men, but those were expensive and impossible to get outside of L.A.

Jerry found Eduardo standing behind his tripod. He checked the frame and grinned giddily. "Beautiful, Eduardo."

"Mike's tight on the window with camera B," Eduardo said, pointing out a couple of guys with mullets and backup cameras, "and Dan has an even wider angle for safety."

Jerry's whole body vibrated with anticipation. Christ, this was really about to happen! He raised his voice toward the crew: "Thank you all for your hard work, time, and radness. I couldn't have made this bitchin' movie without you."

He started a round of applause that the crew joined in haphazardly.

"Let's get a move on," Eduardo said, nodding toward the spears of sunlight poking out the side of the house. The sun was about to disappear behind the neighborhood houses; this was their last chance to grab a beautiful magic hour shot.

Jerry unclipped the walkie-talkie at his belt and thumbed the mic. "Lydia, is Malachi ready?"

***

Claire heard Jerry's voice squawk from Lydia's walkie and reached for the helmet in Malachi's hands. "Quick," she whispered, "before there's time to change anything."

Lydia glanced toward the two of them, standing on each side of the bike. "All set?"

Sweat drizzled down Malachi's face and he struggled to take a breath. Claire jumped in, "Roger that!"

As Lydia relayed the okay, Claire dragged her eyes along the room. A wooden ramp stretched twenty feet across the beige carpet at a gradual angle that ascended to the middle of the window. The glass pane had been set carefully on a bed of pillows.

The breakaway pane was made of spun sugar. It would shatter with ease at the moment of impact, spraying shards that weren't sharp enough to cut skin or eyeballs but looked great on-camera.

After that, Jerry had assured Malachi, it was a short ride down the sloping rooftop, slightly bumpy from the tiles, then a twenty-foot drop onto the mats. Crew members were standing by to catch him, if needed—although, Eduardo had remarked, that sounded like it would cause *more* injuries.

Malachi had been terrified from the instant Jerry told him what he had planned. But Claire thought it sounded excellent—the ultimate wild ride for Danger Claire. She knew there was a risk of bodily harm, but she'd made bigger jumps off higher elevations and strutted away unscathed. This time, at least, there was a camera to capture it.

"We're rolling, Malachi," Lydia said. "Whenever you're ready, go for it."

Claire grabbed the helmet and yanked it out of Malachi's sweaty grasp. She swung her leg over the bike frame, realizing too late that the seat had been set for Malachi, who was almost half a foot taller. To reach the pedals, she had to lift off the seat and hover over the top bar in a crouch.

"Claire?" Lydia sputtered at her back. "What are you —?"

Claire snapped the helmet strap under her chin, gripped the handlebars, and kicked off with full force.

The bicycle launched forward, past Malachi and the crew guys with their bulging eyes and hilariously gawking mouths. The front tire bumped on the base of the ramp but it didn't throw off Claire's momentum. She pedaled with all her strength, building speed as the bike cruised along the wooden ramp, angling upward and the glass was coming closer and faster, the window filling with the cul-de-sac below and she saw the C-camera guy with his shaggy mullet and then the bike was arching at a steeper angle, pointing her straight toward the sky and her legs pumped like machine pistons and she braced herself as the glass came straight for her—

***

Jerry heard Lydia's voice crackle from his belt, high-pitched and frantic: "Claire's on the bike!"

He looked up at the window. Breath shot from his lungs like he'd been punched. The helmet appeared at the bottom of the window and then the bike. He caught just a glimpse of Claire's blonde hair fluttering behind her before she hit the glass. Time slowed to a cinematic crawl as the window spiderwebbed and for a fraction of a heartbeat that felt like minutes, Jerry prayed the glass was too strong and Claire would bounce off it, dazed but unharmed. He could scream at her for being stupid and reckless, all the while relieved that she was alive.

But the glass fractured like it was supposed to. The window exploded outward, a spray of jagged shards shimmering in the sunbeams. It was beautiful and horrifying and made Jerry's heart stop.

Claire shot out of the window with the front end pointed too high—he was sure she'd overshoot the roof entirely and land in the driveway. Then she angled the front wheel down with precise control. The tire bounced off the sloping roof. Skidded slightly on a loose tile. Claire straightened it out, wrangling the handlebars with the expertise of a motocross rider. She pointed the bike straight and rode it right off the roof.

Jerry was moving without realizing it. He darted across the lawn, propelled by a spike of adrenaline. He kept his eyes on the roof, following the bike's trajectory, but his peripheral vision was attuned to the attic. Quivering blackness emerged through the wall, a dark cloud that plunged faster than the bike was racing over the rooftop.

The rear tire left the roof as the front end dipped downward, aimed at the mat tower. Claire released the handlebars and seemed to hang in mid-air like a spacewalking astronaut—for just a moment, before she toppled earthward, head-first.

The Presence swooped down with startling swiftness. Its black fingers reached for the back of Claire's foot with talon-sharp claws.

Jerry reached the mats and jumped to the top in a single vault that he wouldn't have imagined possible without a pole. He landed on the top mat with enough room to launch himself at the Presence.

He was on a collision course with Claire, who looked at him with bulging eyes. If any part of Jerry regretted this intervention, the terror on her face pushed it away. He reached for the sister he'd treated as a nuisance instead of the devoted partner she'd always been.

Jerry caught Claire and embraced her for a hummingbird's flutter, before he pivoted away to position himself between Claire and the ghost. If the Presence wanted to lunge around Jerry to reach its true prize, it had no time for the maneuver. It seemed to accept this inevitability and enfolded its shimmering arms around his body.

In his final moments, Jerry's mouth filled with ash and his nostrils burned with smoke and his vision was consumed by blackness. And then he was gone, along with the Presence.

***

Claire was trying to make sense of the whirlwind of confusion around her when her face smacked the bottom of the swimming pool. Some kind of dark swarm had descended on her with horrifying speed—a cloud of wasps? She couldn't figure any of it out as she rolled off the side of the mats.

Two crew members raced to catch her, but she fell too fast. Claire hit the ground sideways, hearing a snap in her left shoulder that, mercifully, she didn't feel right away.

Eduardo ran to Claire, gasping. "Are you hurt?"

She shook her head, ignoring the numbness spreading along her left arm. "Did you get the shot?"

Eduardo nodded, looking around in confusion. "Where's Jerry?"

Claire sat up and whipped her head around, searching the yard for Jerry. But there was no trace of him—or the black cloud. Had she only imagined its arms and clawed fingers?

Claire scanned the rooftop. The broken window was filled with Lydia and Malachi's concerned faces.

Shrill voices yammered around Claire:

"Was that real?"

"Looked real to me!"

"Should we call the police?"

"*Had* to be special effects!"

She spotted a dark silhouette in the attic window. For an instant, she thought she saw Jerry's face beside it, peering at her—and was he *smiling*? But a second later, the window was empty.

Claire felt a sob welling up in her throat. Although she knew she might never understand what had just occurred, one thing was clear: they had it on film.

Like Jerry always wanted.

The Committee
Emie Baines

England 1930

As the train pulled away from the station I re-read the disturbing letter I had received two days previously from Mrs Brookes, housekeeper to my old Uncle Oswald who lived in the country.

As a boy, in the school holidays, I spent time with Uncle Oswald, benefiting from fresh air and exercise as he took me walking on the large estate with its dark foreboding woodland where he had lived all his life. In autumn we would ramble through crisp brown leaves fallen from the trees which towered over us, their bare branches entwined like old bony fingers. There he would educate me on all types of insect which could be seen just above the damp soil. I was aware, that, when it came to the natural world, my uncle's knowledge knew no bounds. He would also indulge himself, and me, in spine tingling stories from around the world which would terrorise any young mind. Heart pounding, I would nervously watch out for terrifying creatures I feared would emerge from the dark in our secluded surroundings. Even though I always felt safe by his side, if he had related some of his stories to others, outrageously claiming to believe them as he did with me, they would have said he was delusional and needed to be admitted to the asylum. When the letter arrived from Mrs Brookes, it informed me that that was indeed what had happened. The asylum, a dismal place where the deranged are held, isolated from the outside world, was now where my uncle Oswald resided. Whatever had happened to have had him admitted, I only hoped he would be helped there, for all our sakes. So leaving London and my work as a physician to investigate further what had happened to him, I made my way to the large house that held so many memories. And to a most extraordinary and unexpected series of events.

* * *

Grateful to breathe in the air, I stepped out onto the platform. Everything was as it ever was at the familiar station, people rushed about as usual, eager to get to one destination or another.

"Gus, over here!" Mrs Brookes shouted above the crowds waving a stout gloved hand in the air.

It was good to see her, but knew from her letter that whatever had happened involving my uncle, she had been clearly upset, so decided not to push the subject just yet.

We took our usual route, passing through the village with the medieval church, its stained-glass windows lit up with candlelight, trying to battle against the foreboding winter afternoon. I glanced at the familiar sight of the large yew tree standing at the far side of the graveyard which had been there as long as I could remember, always watching and foreboding. Near the entrance, we encountered Reverend Payne taking his usual afternoon walk. Uncle Oswald had accumulated a number of friends from the village who appreciated spending evenings being entertained by his memories of ancient tribes through his travels around the world, and guests always included Reverend Payne. Even though Payne frowned upon what he called 'The bloodthirsty ways of the ancestors', he was always none the less fascinated to hear what my uncle had to say about the near extinct tribes he had encountered throughout his life. Being too young to attend these late-night gatherings, I would sneak downstairs after dinner and listen at the door of the drawing room where everyone had gathered for brandy and cigars, and where Uncle Oswald would begin his memoirs. In the hallway, with its walls of flickering gas light, I heard him tell of his many archaeological digs in faraway lands. After a while I was always caught by Mrs Brookes and promptly sent back to bed, much to my disappointment.

"It's good to see you again Augustus!" the reverend said, looking over his small round spectacles perched on the end of his nose. I noticed a number a deep scratches on the side off his left cheek and wondered about the cause. Perhaps he had been caught in the brambles while tending to the trees in the graveyard.

I tipped my hat towards him in greeting, amused at the use of my full Christian name and hoped he wouldn't try and persuade me to attend church on my stay. I have never been a church going man but someone who examines the bodies of the living, working with physical matter and trying to work out how it functions, so at the time, had no interest in the saving of what he would call the soul. I had heard frequently, my patients talk of going to another place they believed they would enter when they neared the end of their lives, but to me it was too fantastical and merely the final hope of a dying being. As far as I was concerned, the dead were only an array of decaying bones unaware of their own past existence, so was relieved when Mrs Brookes spoke to him only fleetingly.

"Can't stop now Reverend, things to do!" Mrs Brookes she with a smile as we hurried on to the house and to an event that, as I have already hinted at, would change me completely.

* * *

In the vast high-ceilinged dining room, myself and Mrs Brookes sat down to dinner, a candelabra on the table between us to spread a little light. I had put a piece of music on the gramophone to try and help us relax a little, which seemed to do the trick. We dined on a plateau of vegetables and a small joint of beef, rare, and bloody, it was the way Uncle Oswald liked it, and so it was the way Mrs Brookes always prepared it. It had always been my uncle's job to carve the meat, but as there was an empty chair at our table, it was down to me. The large dining room window with its long velvet curtains that I remembered so well was open so we could take in the night air. Halfway through carving I heard a hissing sound. I had first thought it was the sticking of the recording on the gramophone, then realised it was coming from outside. Hearing it again, it made my blood run cold. Mrs Brookes hadn't seemed to have been bothered by it. I put it down to the wind rustling the branches of the trees and continued to carve the meat.

"Tell me all about your work in London," she said as we ate.

"I will Mrs Brookes, but we really have to discuss what happened here first. I was shocked to receive your letter."

"Oh, it was awful! Oh Gus, I can't talk about it right now, I really can't," she replied, placing her knife and folk on her plate unable to continue with her food.

After dinner, I took the candelabra and made my way to the library to choose a book to read over my stay. Climbing the creaking staircase, further memories of being in the house in my younger days came flooding back to me, times when every day had been an adventure. I was sad my uncle wasn't there to share my thoughts. I stopped on the top stair. It was dark on the landing with its large oak doors leading to different rooms. A sudden ruffling sound was coming from behind the library door and there was a distinct movement from inside the room. I heard light footsteps. At that moment I felt very alone and nervous of who I might be confronted with on entering. A beam of light appeared underneath the door. It disappeared then appeared once more. On hearing the ruffling sound again, I my breath and slowly opened the door, the bottom scraped against the worn carpet. Amongst the aroma of dusty books, there was a strong smell of rotting foliage, although the window was fully open and the wind was gently blowing through. Stepping inside I was immediately thrown back onto the floor; a mass of black feathers covered my face. I had dropped the candelabra, luckily the candle flames only singed the carpet slightly. Panic overwhelmed me and I couldn't breathe. Eventually, scrambling to my feet, it was then that I saw them. I felt more fear than I ever had in my entire life.

Vultures! There were at least eight of them looking down on me, all glowing, transparent. They were *phantoms!*

After their attack, the sinister looking creatures flew up to the wooden shelves of the bookcases. I wondered then if madness ran in the family and was revealing itself in *me*. But yet, it all seemed very real. The birds were in the form of shining white lights with dark patterns on their wings. They appeared so at home; it was I who was the intruder in the room. There was silence between us as I continued to stare at them, and they at me. Wanting to run back out of the door, I was frightened if I made a sudden move, they would swoop down and attack me again, this time tearing into me with their sharp beaks and talons until I ended up a bloody corpse on the floor.

Feeling a bony hand on my shoulder, I jumped.

"It's wonderful that you've come back again Gus." I quickly turned, surprised. "It's... good to see you too Uncle!" I stuttered, wondering why Mrs Brookes hadn't mentioned Uncle Oswald had been allowed to come home for the day, and why he had not joined us for dinner. His face lit up as I looked into his ageing rheumy eyes.

"How are you?" I asked, in a sympathetic tone.

"I'm happy you've finally met my friends," he said with a grin.

It was a relief he was aware of the shimmering phantoms too.

My uncle walked to the window. The vultures flew over and stared out of it with him, their loose plumage filling air as they tried to land, some finally settling, one on each of his shoulders, the rest hovered on the window ledge, salivating as they looked towards the fields in the distance where, as the sun was going down a few sheep still grazed and lambs played.

It was as if Uncle Oswald and the vultures were in their own world and I was watching the scene purely as an observer. Tearing my eyes away from them for a moment, I saw the room displayed pictures of the Mayan tribe of South America. They hung on the sides of the bookcases alongside framed photographs of the archaeological trips my uncle had been on. On one of the shelves stood an array of wooden carvings depicting what I understood to be Mayan warriors, as savages. Man turning against man disturbed me, and I wondered why such things fascinated my uncle so much, but only for a moment, nothing had ever really surprised me about my enigma of a relative.

"When did you first see the vultures Uncle?"

"I have always been aware of the Committee," he told me.

"The Committee?"

"When vultures are perched as they are now, they're called a Committee. The ones here now have revealed themselves to us for a reason. The Mayan people thought the vulture symbolised death and the spiritual world, bringing knowledge about that world to those who needed it," he explained.

"But this is outrageous! They appear real, but ghostly! It's not possible!"

"Nothing can separate us from those who have passed over Gus, stories about the dead coming back to visit us are not merely legend."

It was then I realised that the beliefs of others, including my own patients in their final days, with their claims of a life after death, were no more fantastical than what I believed I was seeing at that moment. The birds flew back to their perches where they moved from side to side in a dipping motion, their talons curled around the wood. I stepped back nervously.

"There's no danger Gus," my uncle said, trying to bring some ease to the room.

But again I imagined them ripping through the muscle and intestines of some unfortunate victim. They stretched their bodies so they stood tall, hunched their shoulders and pointed their long necks in my direction, again glaring at me with small beady eyes which told me not to come any closer. When eventually they seemed to relax and showed no further threat, I started to feel less nervous in their presence. Vultures, of course have a cursed name, coming from their need to scavenge other dead creatures, but once I got used to being there with them, although still wary, they were becoming fascinating. The fact that I saw them too brought a smile to my uncle's face as he walked towards me. Perhaps if he had told me about them before I would never have believed him, as to me, it would have defied logic that such things existed. But even though what I saw before me made no sense, it seemed I had no choice but to accept it.

"Why, Uncle, out of all the rooms in the house, are they attracted to the library?" I enquired.

"Like my books, they are full of knowledge and wisdom, so they're comfortable surrounded by such things," he replied.

Soon the vultures became even more at ease in my presence, and being so engrossed in the spectacle of the vultures; I hadn't noticed that my uncle had left the room. He must have closed the door quietly behind him so as not to unnerve the birds. Daring to turn my back on the creatures, I grabbed a book on Maya culture from one of the bookshelves. When I turned back, to my amazement, they too were gone.

* * *

"I'll make us some warm milk to help us sleep," Mrs Brookes said as I passed her on my way to the living room.

Still stunned by the vultures I had encountered in the library, I tried to push them to the back of my mind. If I believed I had seen such things I was no medical man of any worth. But I *had* seen them. Uncle Oswald had always seen them too.

Still, none of it made sense. And did Mrs Brookes know the vultures inhabited the place? I decided not to mention anything about it, in fear of bringing on hysteria.

I made myself comfortable and opened the book on the Mayan's to see pictures of ancient buildings covered with trees and my thoughts returned to my uncle, a man who had lived his life as an explorer and someone to look up to and be admired. I hoped he would join me in the living room for a brandy later so I could ask him all about his time in South America and ask him again about the birds.

The telephone rang in the hall. Mrs Brookes bounded up from the kitchen to answer it. She spoke in her secretarial voice as she did every time she lifted the receiver. I heard her gasp. Then she started to weep.

"What is it Mrs Brookes? I asked entering the hallway.

"That was the asylum...Your uncle... A heart attack. I'm sorry!" she blurted out.

I stood opened mouthed realising that only a short while ago in the library, my uncle had visited me from beyond the grave. And the vultures, on disappearing, had almost certainly followed him back into the ether. An icy sensation ran through my body. I felt as though if I tried to move, it would be like moving through treacle. The revelation of encountering my elderly relative from another realm had stunned me. And again, such a thing defied all logic. I decided to keep it from Mrs Brookes so as not to appear to be the second person in the household to have gone insane.

* * *

Propping myself up in bed, again I read about how the Maya often sacrificed their fellow men. Used to saving lives, rather than sending people to their deaths, it made uncomfortable reading, so I turned down the small oil lamp next to me and lay down to sleep.

During the night I was woken by hissing sounds and knew the vultures had returned to the library. Listening to the flapping of wings, I knew they were restless and couldn't help but get out of bed and make my way across the landing, it was as if they were calling me.

Entering the room again, the palms of my hands clammy with sweat, I stood, transfixed. The birds were hovering in a line across the width of the library, each one touching the tip of the another's wing. Through the open window the moon shone, lighting up the otherwise black vast space. One by one they flew out into the night. I was aghast. Running to the window I saw the row of feathered bodies glow in the air. I stood trembling in fear, but there was also something captivating about the whole thing. Looking down at the outside of the house, roots had sprouted from the ground and soon branches with large leaves spread out along the sides of the wall. I had seen it all before in the book I had been reading, in the photographs of the forests which had shown buried temples. Up above, the vultures hovered in the infinite sky facing the moon, eventually disappearing into the distance. Looking down at the outside of the house again I saw the forest had disappeared. I was both astonished and bewildered, not knowing how it had all happened, I only knew it had.

* * *

Pushing the events of the previous night to the back of my mind, I put on my clothes and headed downstairs. Hearing the clinking of china cups from the living room, I entered to find Mrs Brookes sitting opposite Reverend Payne.

"Oswald picked out his own spot, facing the yew tree in the graveyard I believe," Mrs Brookes said to Payne, dabbing her eyes with a handkerchief.

"Don't worry, I'm aware of his wishes. Although I think his other request is a bit unusual to say the least, but it's possible," he replied.

Mrs Brookes suddenly realised I was in the room. "Oh good morning Gus!"

"What else did my uncle request?"

Payne squirmed in his chair. "Well, erm...."

"Go on!" I said, now annoyed at the secretiveness about recent events from both Payne and Mrs Brookes since my arrival.

Payne continued, uncomfortably. "Oswald's gravestone will be quite a spectacle, he stated there should be a large carving above his name."

"A carving of...?"

"A vulture! With wings spread wide," he replied in a displeased tone. I laughed loudly, knowing that would be a fitting tribute to Uncle Oswald.

Once the reverend left, Mrs Brookes finally told me how my uncle had come to be certified mad. For days he'd been walking through the house flapping his arms up and down, a hissing sound coming from his mouth, finally perching on the edge of the sofa to stare straight ahead for hours at a time, his eyes reduced in size, and looking menacing. She had ran all the way to the church to get Reverend Payne to help, and upon seeing him walk through the door, my uncle went for him, neck outstretched, and finger nails clawing at his face. Mrs Brookes and Payne eventually tackled my uncle to the ground, and he had lain there ridged with fear, looking up at the ceiling. I could only imagine the scene of upset for all involved. Mrs Brookes wept into her handkerchief once more at the memory of the ordeal. She had been with my uncle for a long time, they had been friends and she was lost without him.

* * *

At the graveside, Reverend Payne, myself, Mrs Brookes and my uncle's friends from the village, said our goodbyes. The air was still as we stood, silently, lost in our memories of such an extraordinary man . As the church clock struck the hour, we were brought back to the present.

Throwing a handful of soil down on top of the coffin deep in the ground, I heard the familiar ruffling of feathers. I glanced over at the yew tree opposite to see a familiar sight, a glowing vulture perched on a bare branch. Within minutes the tree was full of them looking down at us. Suddenly they disappeared. Then looking up at the sky I saw something that took my breath away. I was shocked, but at the same time elated to see the vultures flying together towards the heavens, and in the middle, arms outstretched, was my uncle, being safely delivered to his rest.

* * *

Time marches on, and I am now retired from my work as a London doctor, where, whenever I was about to lose a patient who claims an over worldly faith, I assured them I was a believer too. My experience at my former childhood home made me a more understanding physician, knowing it wasn't all about curing the physical, but also about not denying the existence of the soul, helping those under my care to go with peace. And as I head towards old age at great speed, I do confess, I wonder if the vultures will come back for me when my time comes, and if they do, I hope Uncle Oswald will be there too.

Ongweias and the Stone Coats
Ken Leland

He told the Haudenosaunee shaman it was one thousand, seven hundred, ninety-two years since the Settlers' only Prophet was born. Coohcoocheeh was interested in such things. Often she asked him what Settlers believed, why they did thus and so.

The old woman sighed. "Aaron, my son, that was so long ago. Aren't they sad no new voice has spoken?"

"Settlers suppose he answered all questions back then. A new prophet is unneeded."

Coohcoocheeh studied him closely, then lowered her eyes. "It is not meet to say such things with a quiet face."

Aaron leaned to kiss her brow. "Istena, I'm not teasing. I don't understand it either."

***

In the Haudenosaunee tongue, Aaron often spoke of Coohcoocheeh as 'Istena,' or 'Mother,' yet she was not the woman who gave him life. His own dear parents were Settlers who lived many days east near a great water falls at Niagara.

A year ago, in the spring of 1791, Aaron had joined the Askin Trading Post, located at the confluence of the Maumee and Auglaize Rivers. His mentor in the fur trade was John Norton, the factor of that place. A young Neshnabek named Toghtarask was Aaron's friend and the post's principal traveler among the First Nations.

In this second year of apprenticeship, Aaron took sole responsibility for trade until Spring; but in fact, little needed doing since local Nations had already scattered to late autumn hunting grounds. Toghtarask and Aaron helped Norton load pack horses to return to his winter home. Norton would trek south to the Scioto River, to live with the Shawnee woman who was his beloved companion.

As red leaves drifted upon Auglaize waters, Coohcoocheeh blessed Norton, then kissed him goodbye. With a firm handshake, Norton bid Aaron and Toghtarask farewell. Gray clouds filled the sky as the pack train plodded south along the Auglaize trail.

***

One cold dawn, almost two weeks after Norton left, Aaron awoke with vague unease. He stumbled to open the trading post shutters while his dream faded; images of an arduous journey, towards a place, for a purpose, he'd already forgotten. Through second storey windows, he saw Coohcoocheeh across the Maumee River, three hundred paces distant. She stood on the riverbank beneath yellowing willows from hence she'd piqued his disquiet. In growing light, she signed broadly. "Come soon. Bring Toghtarask."

Toghtarask called from his first floor bedroom. "Aaron! Did she wake you too? What does she want?"

They tramped down log steps to the river pier. After lifting and rolling a canoe to empty freezing night rain, they paddled a few score paces along the Auglaize before entering the Maumee. Coohcoocheeh's cabin lay on the Maumee shore, two hundred heartbeats away. Aaron pulled them across while Toghtarask angled their canoe against the current. After sliding into the ice-edged riverbank, Toghtarask braced the canoe as his friend leapt ashore. "Aaron, have we've done something wrong?"

"Brother! How should I know?"

They gathered at her table, while Coohcoocheeh spoke quietly. "Word came to me in the night." Sipping roasted chicory, the young men glanced to one another. No night messenger had ridden the river trail.

"Norton has hurt himself. I dreamt something about an axe. His leg is badly broken and must be set and bound."

Toghtarask grimaced. "Who will hunt for his family this winter?"

Coohcoocheeh nodded and refilled their cups. "Yes, you understand."

"Istena, is there no one close by to help them?"

"No, Aaron. There is only Norton's companion, Tikecomme, her children and aged parents. They are several day's travel from other Shawnee."

"A lonely camp makes for good hunting," Toghtarask

said, "but help is far if needed."

Coohcoocheeh stood and brought a woven sack to the table. Inside were small clay pots. "I have prepared salves, but I do not believe Tikecomme and her father can set his leg unaided. A strong, young man is needed."

Aaron reached to touch his friend's shoulder. "Toghtarask, would you watch over the trading post until I return?"

"I will, Brother."

Istena reached to hug Aaron. "Thank you, my son."

***

It was snowing that morning when Aaron loaded a travois with bags of jerky and dried peas. He oiled his long rifle and they departed, the chestnut mare and Aaron, walking for the Scioto River Country.

Two days out, they broke through thin ice on Blanchard's Creek. Chestnut saved him. As he clung to her reins, she angled sideways to safety, pulling Aaron from bone-numbing water. Though safe on the creek bank, his limbs burned while he changed cold, wet leathers for dry. Soon a fever grew. Disoriented by his immersion, he became confused and did not realize his danger. Stumbling at sunset, he wandering aimlessly until Mingo hunters discovered him. Grandfather and his three grown sons brought Aaron to their winter camp. In the warmth of the Mingo lodge, gradually he recovered his senses.

After supper, young and old gathered round the lodge fire to hear a story. A boy of eight Summers sat resting his elbow on Aaron's knee while Grandmother told a long humorous tale about Turtle, Partridge and She Wolf, all spending a Winter together. When her story ended, Grandmother said it was time for little ones to go to sleep. The boy beside Aaron sighed. "Now Grandfather will tell a story for grownups. Grandmother says his stories are too scary, so we have to go to bed now."

In dancing firelight, Grandfather's three sons and their companions spooned together beneath blankets. Wrapped in warm furs, Aaron lay on a solitary pallet to listen. Grandfather began a long meandering tale about

Stone Coats, Demons of Cold and Ice; and their rival, Ongweias, an ever-starving Cannibal Spirit. The story rambled on and on, until finally Aaron lost its thread. Some time later, Grandmother returned after rocking her youngest to sleep. She knelt and give Aaron a warm, soothing drink to soften his fever.

"Sleep well, my son. May the Great Spirit watch over you until we meet again."

***

Next morning, the men took the young fur trader to a trail winding south from Blanchard Creek to the Scioto River. One of Grandfather's sons looked to darkening clouds. "In a little while it will snow hard."

"You'll reach the Scioto just at midday," said another.

The third hunter laughed. "If you can tell midday in a blizzard!"

Grandfather put his hand upon Aaron's back. "This track is plain in fine weather, but it skirts a great marsh. Perhaps I should come with you. My legs need a good stretch."

Aaron was young and foolish. He thanked him, no. "Grandfather, I won't lose my way."

With long rifle in hand and Chestnut pulling the heavy travois, they started out. As morning continued, snow began to swirl. A strong southwest wind blew wet flakes into their faces and Chestnut shook her head. The young man tightened the laces on his jacket hood until he could barely see beyond its fur trim. Very soon both were covered in a layer of white, and Aaron knelt to strap on snowshoes. When he looked up again, the trail had disappeared.

Moments before, there were trees ahead, and it would be most welcome to take shelter in a stand of evergreens. With a pat for her neck and a word of encouragement, he led Chestnut to the right, towards dark shadows that became merely a clump of tangled bushes. On the left were tussocks of prairie grass and they walked among them, the mare straining to pull travois poles over icy mounds. The wind blew harder and she lost patience. She wanted to lower her head and lie down. At her jaw, Aaron gripped the bridle tightly to guide Chestnut forward through the storm.

Walking in snowshoes through the blizzard, he was upright and steady, so steady he didn't realize the deepening snow covered a freezing pond. A wide spot between tussocks, what he'd hoped was the trail, turned out to be only crackling rime. Chestnut was startled and lost her footing. Frightened, she tried to back up, only to be caught when the poles dug into the ice. A sharp tug on the bridle captured her attention, and words spoken firmly in her ear, calmed her. Aaron unhitched the litter so she might stand unencumbered. They sought their back trail but it was disappearing fast. After a hundred steps, one could only guess where they'd passed.

They were lost in the Scioto Marsh.

The storm lined Aaron's hood with snow, and most unwisely, he abandoned Norton's winter provisions somewhere behind them. In despair, Aaron stumbled to a halt and peered blindly into white gusts. Chestnut shivered, her head hung low. She tugged gently on the reins, and almost losing hope, he trusted to follow her as the wind pressed against their backs. He prayed her course would lead them out of the swamp.

***

After a time, the storm began to ease, but they were hungry and tired. Ahead were tall, dark shadows that resolved into a stand of spruce trees. The treetops leaned close together to form a swaying cavern. Inside was a campfire where embers gleamed. A wooden frame was fixed just above the fire, strong enough to roast an elk. A small figure sat beside the flames wearing leggings and moccasins, but his chest was bare even in the freezing cold. A line of sharp bones marked the stranger's spine; his skin was stretched tight over a dark forehead and cheeks. While Aaron approached the fire, the creature tapped a riverstone tomahawk against his left palm. Aaron called out. "Halloo the fire. May I join you?"

"Of course. I've been waiting for you, Cousin."

"I am Aaron of the Deer Clan. I've lost my way."

Entering the grotto as snowflakes diminished,

Chestnut baulked with stiffening legs. She would come no closer. Aaron retreated and tied her to a tree branch. He stooped to remove his snowshoes and left his rifle beside them in hopes the bony stranger would put his tomahawk aside.

But he did not.

Again, Aaron walked forward cautiously. He spoke in Shawnee, guessing this person might be of that Nation. "I didn't know I was expected."

"I gambled with hunters, each of us for our heart's desire," the gaunt man replied. "I won." He held out a shallow bowl with peach stones, all five showing the white side up. "I was first to throw five. They went into the storm to seek what I long for."

The fire was warm and inviting, but the emaciated man still patted the stone club slowly against his palm. Aaron looked from side to side into the forest, but other gamblers were nowhere to be seen. Looking back, he couldn't remember in what language the stranger had replied. Aaron then tried Anishinabek. "Uncle, what is your heart's desire?"

"Why it stands before me," the starveling chirped. His body quivered as he stood.

"Uncle, what is your name?" This time Aaron spoke in Haudenosaunee.

The Cannibal Spirit screamed. "Ongweias!"

Ongweias rushed forward, looming ever larger, and with the tomahawk he struck hard against Aaron's hood. Aaron collapsed in a heap, dazed and barely conscious. Ongweias chortled as he dragged his victim to the fire. Gibbering and cackling, he threw his victim on the roasting frame and covered him with thick, binding vines. Aaron feigned death; indeed he could scarcely move after such a blow.

Perhaps Ongweias thought his prey was dead, for the Man Eater did not search him. The monster's tongue smoothed his lips as he watched in anticipation. Soon enough, the coating of snow would melt, the jacket begin to smolder, the youth's flesh to sear, and in only a little time, Ongweias' deepest yearnings would be satisfied.

At the camp's edge, Chestnut snorted. The fiend heard her and darted in that direction. Then, she screamed and strained against her knotted reins. Rearing, she struck out with her front hooves, but Ongweias ducked underneath and raised his tomahawk again. Horse meat would do when man flesh was consumed, his hunger knew no limits. In fear, she broke the leads and galloped away, the Cannibal Spirit bounding in pursuit.

With Ongweias gone, Aaron shook off his torpor and used a knife to cut the vines. He rolled from the spit to snatch up his rifle and snowshoes before plunging into the trees to hide. A few minutes later, he observed Ongweias returning empty-handed, but accompanied by others.

They were three tall figures with white, frosty hair that hung to their shoulders. Each carried a stone-tipped spear and around their chests, front and back, was a thick sheet of ice extending from neck to below the belly. These were Stone Coats, Beings of Cold and Ice, with frozen hearts. Ongweias hurried to the firepit. "Gone! My heart's desire is gone."

"What are you talking about?" the tallest, the Stone Coat Chief, asked.

It has escaped from my fire! The answer to all my longings has disappeared."

The demons turned stiffly to one another, their chins held high by the cylinders encasing each one. Surely, the Man Eater's mind had flown.

The Stone Coat Chief smiled in disdain. "We gambled and lost, but we cannot return an ephemeral spirit to your fire. We'll track down that horse we saw running free. We're leaving now."

"Cheaters! Liars!"

In a rage, Ongweias loomed high again, tall as a spruce tree. He leapt at the Stone Coats, swinging a massive war club. He towered above them, but the Chief thrust up his spear to strike the tomahawk's shaft. Its long wooden handle shattered into frosty splinters. Man Eater staggered beyond range of that life freezing spear.

"We're going, Ongweias. Best you remain here."

As they trudged away, Aaron crept deeper into the

woods, then circled to follow. If they touched Chestnut with a spear, his mission could end only in despair.

***

As clouds parted, the light of late morning grew. From a distance he watched the three Stone Coats chasing his mare along the marsh's edge. They were heavy with ice and could not run swiftly. Without snowshoes, they staggered through crusted snow. They could not bend or tilt their heads to search for tracks. Still, they hunted doggedly, always keeping the horse in sight. Eventually, as they neared the exhausted mare, one demon stood forth and raised his spear horizontally before Chestnut's face. Now she appeared docile, or perhaps so stricken with cold, she could flee no longer. The Stone Coats were careful not to nudge her with their spears as they herded her away. With a sinking heart, Aaron sat upon a log, and although he thought long and hard, there seemed no way to rescue his horse.

As he pondered, strands of tawny vapor drifted over the ground. The flowing wisps gathered before him, grew in strength and form, until a great stag snorted and pawed the snow. Shaking his antlers, Stag slashed the air. "Your friends on the Scioto are in great need. Stone Coats have your horse. The provisions you brought are lost in the marsh. What will you do now?"

"I don't know. These demons are far beyond my strength."

"Is this not the moment to decide which vision to follow?"

"If I fight them, surely I will die."

Again, Stag torn the air with his antlers. "Perhaps, but what do *you* most wish for?"

Aaron paused only a moment. There could be no doubt. "To help my friends."

"Then let that be your guide. Is there a greater gift, a greater vision than to save those you love? Does it really matter whether you die today or many years from now?"

He thought once more. "No, the end is the same. Yet I would have some hope for today. Can you help me?"

"Have you noticed that Stone Coats are able only to

stare straight ahead?" Stag asked.

"Yes."

"In the Chief's medicine bag is a Spirit. Ask where a thing is and that Spirit will point to it. Ask how to do a thing and the Spirit will help you find a way."

"Stag, how can I steal this magic?"

"I've no idea. You'll have to figure that out yourself."

***

Boldly, Aaron followed the demons' trail. The chestnut mare strode ahead slowly, herded from behind and on each side. The Stone Coat Chief was last and most easily approached. At the Chief's waist, Aaron could see a medicine bag dangling from a throng. He bent low, reached out with his knife and cut it loose. The bag fell unnoticed and Aaron fell flat on the snow to cover it. The Demons of Cold tramped on towards their village.

When they were gone, Aaron sat and opened the medicine bag to feel inside. He found only a small, narrow stick. On closer examination, he realized the stick was a shriveled finger. Aaron almost dropped it in surprise. Dumbfounded, he rose onto his knees with the desiccated finger on his palm.

Was this Stag's advice? Complaining aloud, Aaron asked, "What earthly good can a finger be? I don't even know where I left the travois."

Immediately, Finger sprang to attention and seemed to point back into the swamp. Aaron was amazed.

"Can you show me where I left the provisions?"

The upright digit bent at its first joint.

"Does that mean 'Yes'?" Again, Finger bent.

"Show me 'No'." This time Finger wavered from side to side.

"Guide me to the travois." Finger pointed once more.

Following the spirit's directions, Aaron located where he'd strayed into the marsh, and soon thereafter, the travois, quite undisturbed. While the sun rose to midday, he labored to carry everything back to the portage trail, then collapsed in exhaustion atop the bundles.

Having caught his breathe, again Aaron removed Finger from the medicine bag. "Somehow I must get the horse back here without alerting the Stone Coats. How can I do that?"

Finger only lay quivering in his hand.

"Is there a way to do that?"

This time Finger straightened up. At first it bowed, but then it moved from side to side.

"So, I must ask only one question at a time. Can I get the horse back here?"

"Yes," came the bending answer.

"Can I do this without alerting the Stone Coats?"

"No."

Aaron tried again. "Can I succeed in helping my friends?"

"Yes."

"How?" Finger only quivered.

"Arrgh!"

After much agonizing, at last Aaron asked, "Show me how to escape from the Stone Coats with my horse."

This time Finger pointed back into the swamp and led him on a winding path, across many crackling ponds, until finally they drew near the Winter Demons' camp.

"Finger, is this the path I must follow to escape these horrors?"

"Yes."

From a hiding place, Aaron could see Chestnut tied to a post outside the Stone Coat lodge. A fire heated a waist-high, clay water pot outside the western door. Seemingly, the demons planned to boil their dinner. Inside the lodge, they argued loudly who should have the privilege of slaughtering the mare.

One voice asserted, "I saw her first. That honor should be mine."

"No, I captured her. She is my prize."

"Neither of you can kill without freezing the horse into a block of ice. Only the Spirit that lives in my medicine bag can show us how."

After hearing this, Aaron looked at Finger. "What should I do?"

Finger pointed first to Chestnut, then to a long stone club the demons used to grind corn, and finally, to the steaming caldron.

A frantic cry came from the lodge. "What's happened to my medicine bag? Someone stole it!"

Aaron rushed into the camp, untied the mare and gave her a stinging slap on the rump. "Run, Chestnut!" When she fled, Aaron struggled to raise the stone mallet to his shoulder. The three demons burst from the lodge, and he scurried to position himself behind the caldron.

He lifted Finger aloft. "Look what I have!"

The Stone Coat Chief stomped closer, shouting, "Give it back."

Aaron swung the club hard against the clay pot and water erupted just as the chief lunged forward, his spear extended. He slipped down into the water, now pouring over his feet, and suddenly was transfixed in ice.

"Get him, Brothers! Freeze his bones."

Aaron fled and the other two demons lumbered after him. Aaron soon discovered the ice covered Stone Coats were faster than he'd thought possible. Veering onto the swamp trail, the swifter demon was only a pace or two behind. Tantalizingly, Aaron's head and shoulders bobbed and weaved just ahead of him. As the demon began to extend his spear, Aaron reached the middle of a snow covered pond. His wide-spreading snowshoes held, but the driving legs of the heavy monster plunged through, dropping the demon into water waist-deep. Instantly, the entire pond froze to the bottom, trapping the flailing horror in solid ice.

"Careful, Brother! Watch for the ponds."

The third Stone Coat slid across the rock-hard surface in close pursuit. This last demon must have guessed, but could not lower his chin to see, how his brother broke through into the swamp. Shrewdly, the last brute ran parallel to Aaron's trail, thinking to avoid more freezing traps.

Aaron crossed pond after pond, while his tormenter ran safely aside, beyond their edges. Nearing the last snow-covered pool, Aaron's strength began to fail. He almost gave up hope. Surely, he was about to die.

Ahead to the left, antlers swayed above alder bushes.

Desperately, Aaron abandoned Finger's trail and broke towards the bushes. The last demon also swerved left to pace him, and unwittingly, blundered onto the final trap. Again, ice shattered to pitch the weighty terror neck deep into instantly solid water.

With heaving sobs, Aaron staggered on a few more steps, then collapsed onto a snowy mound. His lungs rasping, he could hear the outraged Stone Coat screaming for his brothers to bring stone mallets to crack the ice. In the distance were the bawls of the second Stone Coat, and farther still, those of the Chief, each caught firmly in ice cold malice.

"I'll give you no help, not on my life." Aaron muttered as he limped away. He found Chestnut standing beside the travois, waiting patiently for him to load the provisions. Then, they hurried onward to find the Scioto River.

***

The blizzard returned as dusk fell. Pine copses were close and they were about to choose one for shelter, when before them, a glow floated shoulder high in swirling snowflakes. A Wyandot warrior guarded the trail. Affixed to his staff, he carried a burning bowl of grease-soaked, wooden chips. Beyond the warrior, Aaron could see a string of floating fires.

"Welcome home, Brother. Follow the lights."

Passing each glow as darkness cloaked the land, they finally reached a village. In a hollow, bonfires burned bright where women baked turkey and venison. Children chased one another down a creek path, calling out to Aaron in welcome. Here, mighty Scioto was only a rivulet a child might jump across.

A Wyandotte Grandmother approached to tuck his arm beneath hers. "Come inside, my son. Young folk will tend all your needs."

And indeed, two boys led Chestnut to a warm stable with summer cut grass. Grandmother took him to her family lodge and opened wide the eastern door. The wigwam was tall and comfortably warm, though snow fell noiselessly without. At three hearths, burning branches pulsed red in the night.

A young woman pulled off his sweat stained jacket and brought a clay bowl of warm water. "Wash and take your place beside a fire."

Grandfather nodded in greeting. "We thank the Great Spirit for preserving you this day. May He shield us all until we meet again."

Aaron feasted, then closed his eyes to fall into the Dream of Life.

At morning's light, he woke to a great chill. No furs covered his body or cushioned his head. Long dead ashes lay in hearth rings beside him. Shivering on hard dirt, he rolled onto his back and saw a gaping, fire-ravaged hole in the sagging roof. Flurries drifted into the ruined wigwam.

His long rifle was safe on the ground beside him, and resting on its stock was a dry brown twig. He found more lodges outside, each with fire blackened poles painted in hoar frost. Long-suffering Chestnut stood unhobbled beside the stream, the travois and food bundles beside her.

The destroyed village had been abandoned long ago.

***

Following the Scioto eastward, and then a little south, they reached the sixth creek that flowed into the widening river. There, they turned north, and with a last few flakes at midday, Chestnut and Aaron traveled along a rock filled wash. Clouds began to part and the fragrance of a cherry wood fire drifted along the cut.

Smoke sang a Shawnee homecoming song when he reached the top of the draw.

Norton, Aaron's friend, was there, resting in sunlight at the camp's edge. Sorely injured, Norton raised himself onto an elbow and called a greeting from the pallet where he lay. His companion, Tikecomme, and her children scurried from their home to fall upon Aaron's neck. Her father and mother wrung his hand and embraced him.

Tears sprang from Aaron's eyes. "With the Great Spirit's help, I escaped Ongweias, foxed the Stone Coats and stole a magic Finger. Last night, I feasted in the Village of the Departed. Dear friends, let us put Norton's leg to rights. I will hunt for everyone until he is healed. I cannot say how happy I am to see you all, above ground and in broad daylight."

Haunting
Mark A Fisher

what then will the well dressed ghost be wearing
to the festivals of mist and shadows
with every sightless eye still staring
awaiting for anything to expose

dark buried secrets taken to the grave
now get whispered about within these halls
to still be remembered is all they crave
no longer to dance melancholy balls

with all the other lost forgotten souls
that would not or could not cross the river
to Tartarus' or Elysium's shoals
their long eternity to deliver

now merely shadows that are still clinging
as the brash alarum bells are ringing

Last Confession Of A Luftwaffe Ace
Douglas Kolacki

Journal of Major Johannes Kellner, Jagdgeschwader 5./JG 11
121 aerial victories, winner of the Knight's Cross with Oak Leaves

I

I wonder now: Why did my own face never appear on that Fortress?

The American's did. Perhaps I should begin with him.

That morning at 1000 hours we heard the alert, "Concentrations of enemy aircraft on Dora-Dora." Three divisions of bombers approaching from the direction of Great Yarmouth.

Based on Germany's northern frontier between Holland and Denmark, we were the first line of defense against the RAF and U.S. 8th Air Force droning in day after day, night after night, raining down bombs with the unrelenting, clockwork regularity we Germans were usually known for.

Our formations in Holland tracked the bombers over Amsterdam, then above the southern tip of Ijssel Bay. When they were over Rheine, the order rang from the loudspeakers along the field: "Entire squadron to take off. Entire squadron to take off."

We sprinted out to our Messerschmitts. Engines sputtered to life, canopies slammed shut, and we roared upward.

I was flying a BF-109G, which performs well at high altitude and carries a centrally-mounted 20mm cannon along with its 7.92mm machine guns. Armed with those, you can bring down almost anything with only a few hits, and I had 119 kills marked on my rudder along with the Knight's Cross.

While I climbed, my radio crackled. "Heavy babies in

sector Gustav-Quelle. Go to Hanni-eight-zero."

"Victor, victor," I acknowledged.

The ground shrank away into a patchwork of green, rolling hills and the blue harbor. Except for our base, there was no sign that any war was being fought. The woolen clouds passed and made a white carpet over the earth as I passed 20,000, then 25,000 feet. Here was where the war machines clashed, but unlike ground combat, which tore up everything in its path, these left no scars or destruction in the air. The sky waited patiently as we men scrapped, and when it was over and the fires burned below, went right on with its peace.

At 30,000 feet I sighted the telltale vapor trails below and to the west. They came into view, gleaming silver Fortresses, hundreds of them, lined up in ranks stretching back plane after plane until they seemed to disappear over the horizon. All wings level, all bearing the white star on fuselages with fifty-caliber machine guns in eight positions. These also had fighter escort, Thunderbolts and Lightnings wheeling and spiraling above and alongside the heavies.

One of our Focke-Wulf squadrons broke away. Their orders were to engage the fighters and keep them occupied while we in the 109's intercepted the Fortresses. My wingman, *Feldwebel* Beck, followed closely as we approached. He played the accordion and often entertained us with lively dance tunes.

Breathing steadily through my oxygen mask, I thought of *Oberst* Schallhorn, our squadron commander. Mission after mission he attacked the heavies head-on, shooting down twenty-nine and boosting his overall total to three hundred and five. He had been confirmed for the Knight's Cross with Diamonds--the highest award--when a Thunderbolt finally got the better of him. He rode his crate down, managing to belly-land in a field before it exploded.

Choosing a group of bombers on the right flank, I approached from the front. You close with alarming speed, and in the few seconds I had I aimed, fired my cannon and screamed overhead, inverting as I climbed. I could not see the result.

Swinging around to the left in a wide arc, I meant to overtake the formation and then bank for a second frontal attack. Beck followed. Bomber after bomber passed by on my left, steady on course, never wavering or drifting. Sparks twinkled from some of them as the waist gunners fired. Pushing the throttle forward, my propeller thrumming, I noticed the peculiar artwork painted on each bomber's nose.

We had all seen them, of course. Inevitably these were often women in pinup poses, scantily clad with exaggerated busts, waving the Stars and Stripes or riding bombs like bucking horses. LIBERTY BELLE winked at me as I passed, wearing a half-unzipped flight jacket and a pilot's cap; ALUMINUM OVERCAST showed a girl in a bathing suit sitting on a lightning bolt. MISS JOLLY ROGER held a cutlass, wearing a tricorn on her head but nothing else above her waist. Not all were women, however. The NINE O NINE had a Minuteman from the American Revolution riding a bomb and thumbing his nose. The YE OLDE PUB, then the THUNDER BIRD, passed by next.

Passing the last of these, I cleared the formation's vanguard--or thought I did--

Another Fortress arrested my view. Unpainted like the rest, four propellers humming, identical in every way except for its own artwork.

This airplane was called GRIM REAPER.

The capital letters, predictably crimson, glowed as if red hot. They curled up at each end into a semicircle, where they framed--but this was surprising. One would expect a grinning skeleton in a hooded robe holding a scythe (or perhaps, in this case, a bomb), but there was nothing of the sort, not even a hooded pinup girl. The fearsome letters framed, rather, the face of a perfectly ordinary-looking young man, square-jawed, with black hair and a spit curl like Superman. He looked no more like a "grim reaper" than that cartoon hero. A flight jacket clothed his shoulders before the rest of him disappeared into the glaring letters beneath.

--I jolted. Beck was shouting at me over the pops and

static on the radio. Fighter pilots have a bad habit of over-talking, but now I saw the reason for all his noise: my speed had slowed to match that of the bombers. In seconds gunners would make mincemeat of us.

I gave my head a violent shake and gunned my 109's throttle. The GRIM REAPER soon fell behind. The letters still glowed in my mind's eye, as if I had gazed too long into the sun. I scowled. There was no *time* for mistakes like this! We were sixty planes against hundreds as it was, and even an instant's lapse could mean suffering Schallhorn's fate.

I was starting to come around for the frontal attack when Beck broke away, vanishing into a cloud cover. What the...? And then I saw why: three Thunderbolts were swooping down on my tail.

I wrenched my crate into a corkscrew-climb as bullets whistled by. Then came the *woomf-woomf-woomf* of fifty-caliber rounds hitting my aircraft. My instrument panel shattered and I smelled smoke.

One of the Thunderbolts overshot me, roaring past. Instantly I squeezed the trigger. My guns hammered and the rounds flew out, looking like a string of pearl necklaces. They nailed him square in the fuselage. Smoke trailed, then poured behind him as yellow flame licked from the engine cowling. The fire spread to the fuselage and it burned more fiercely; the fuel line must have been feeding it.

Despite most of my instruments now gone, I still had control of my crate. The smoke smell was clearing, or at least wasn't increasing. The Yank, however, had not bailed out. Easing forward, I pulled alongside him. His cockpit was filling with smoke and he was beating on the canopy, trying to get it open. And then--of this I am certain, there is not even a chance for doubt--I recognized him. It was the square-jawed man whose likeness I had seen painted on the Fortress. Even through the gathering smoke it was unmistakable, down to the spit curl sticking out from under his leather flight helmet.

"Get out!" I screamed into my oxygen mask. Foolish of course; he could not hear me. But my guns had shredded his elevators, his canopy was jammed, and he had no control of his aircraft. It remained on a level course, burning as it went, and he was going to burn to death trapped in the cockpit.

Looking around, I saw no one. Unbelievably the other two Yanks had gone, and I was alone with this trapped pilot who was starting to roast alive. A cold nausea took hold of me as I realized what I would have to do.

I fell back and maneuvered behind him, lining him up in my gunsight.

This went against everything we believed in. Destroying a helpless opponent was never done, never even thought about. But this would not be murder, I told myself; it was a mercy killing.

I tightened my mouth...and pressed the trigger.

***

I spoke to no one, save for squadron business, for days afterward.

My gun camera confirmed the mercy killing. My superiors counted it my one hundred and twentieth victory regardless.

In the old days that seemed another age now, I flew my first mission as a newly-minted pilot over Russia. A Soviet IL-2 *Shturmovik* bomber crossed my path and, despite all my nervous hesitancy and fumbling, I somehow shot him down.

Now, in June of 1944, I was going to Berchtesgaden to receive the Knight's Cross with Oak Leaves from our leader himself.

II

Increasing kills add increasing awards to the Knight's Cross: the Oak Leaves, the Swords, and finally the Diamonds. These are all presented by the *Führer*. The top pilots who have won them often keep the diamonds in a separate pouch, in case they are ever shot down. Some, like our *General Der Jagdflieger* Galland, take their chances and wear them anyway.

Four pilots went with me on the train. The night before, we caroused and drank too much--champagne and cognac is a devilish combination under any circumstance--and I shuffled into the mountainside residence with Hartmann, Krupinski, Barkhorn and Wiese in a hung-over fog. My head felt like a concrete block.

While we waited in the corridor, Hartmann saw Hitler's hat hanging on a rack and tried it on. It fell over his eyes, and he joked that the *Führer* had a big head for such a small man. "It must go with the job!" The rest of us laughed. Then he mimicked Hitler giving a speech at Nuremburg, raising his arm in the salute, and we laughed even louder. My stomach was churning and I hoped I would not throw up.

"Gentle-*men?*"

We turned. Hitler's Luftwaffe adjutant, Major von Below, stood giving us a look that would melt steel. Hartmann swayed, but fortunately did not lose his balance.

"If you are finished clowning around," Below said, "you have an audience with the *Führer.*"

Then the Major lifted his eyes at something behind us. "Ah! Schallhorn."

I whirled.

For a moment I forgot my sickness. Then it returned threefold. I swayed, lost my balance, and Barkhorn had to grab and steady me.

It was really he, *Oberst* Schallhorn. Or rather, what had been him. Someone gasped, Barkhorn turned green, and I was positive I would lose control at last and vomit last night's champagne and cognac all over Hitler's floor. I shivered, and my vision blurred for a few moments.

Schallhorn wore his blue-gray Luftwaffe uniform, as did we all. His Knight's Cross with Oak Leaves and Swords adorned the front of his collar beneath a face that had been destroyed, yet somehow retained its life. He wore his cap, but it tilted at an odd angle. Somewhere in the back of my mind I guessed it was because his head had lost some of its shape. We gathered around him as he stood looking rumpled, like he had shrunken inside his uniform and was now too small for it, the sleeves covering part of his hands, the trouser cuffs touching the floor. And evidently he had come alone, however he had gotten here, without any nurse or attendant. We would not have been more shocked had an Egyptian mummy walked in.

"Schallhorn!" "We thought you were--" "We heard--" we all babbled at once.

His mouth twitched at the corner. His dull eyes took us in one at a time, unhurriedly. "They...fixed me," he said in a low, hoarse voice, "more or...less." A little drool escaped his mouth as he spoke, but he did not wipe it away; I got the idea that even lifting his hand would take a great effort. He wore no bandages that I saw, unless they were beneath his clothes, but only some two weeks had passed since we had presumed him killed in explosive crash of his 109.

I heard footsteps approaching the instant before Von Below called us to attention. We lined up side by side. Schallhorn approached in a slow shuffle, right foot forward, left, right, each step making a quick scratching sound on the carpet. Von Below regarded him with tight-lipped urgency, *Come on!* as the footsteps neared.

Schallhorn eased into his place at the end, beside Wiese, at the same instant Hitler entered the room.

He wore a gray jacket, his Iron Cross conspicuously pinned to it, and black trousers. His height reminded me of Hartmann's words about "such a small man"--well under two meters. He greeted us one by one, handing us our awards in their presentation boxes, and shook each man's hand. His handshake was weak, more like a woman's. When he came to Schallhorn, Schallhorn only looked at the box like it was some curious thing, not seeming to understand what it was.

Wiese gave him a nudge. "Schallhorn?" he whispered.

Schallhorn lifted his scarred hands, slowly and carefully as with all his movements, and allowed Hitler to place the box in them. Then Hitler gave his right hand a little pat. "It is a victory for us," Hitler said, "that you are here."

We adjourned to the dining room where waiters glided

out with sausage, bread, and carrot salad. Hitler, who never touched meat, had a spinach salad with fruit and a glass of water. I took off my Knight's Cross to fasten the Oak Leaves to it. The others were doing the same with their new decorations. Schallhorn, however, only studied his Knight's Cross with Diamonds, which he had set in front of his plate, still in its box.

A silence hung over the table. Wine was brought out, but the thought of alcohol sickened me, so I sipped the coffee instead. Forks clinked, men put food in their mouths and chewed, but everyone's attention was on Schallhorn. Even Hitler kept quiet.

Finally Barkhorn spoke. "Schallhorn. It was quite a surprise to see you here, I'm very glad." The rest of us chimed our assent.

Schallhorn gave a slight nod. His meal lay untouched on its plate. "The doctors...wanted to be sure I got...my award."

"The Diamonds," I added, really just to keep the talk going.

"The crash...I remember little of it."

"That is fortunate," said Hartmann.

"Little of...much of anything. Big gaps." Schallhorn looked down at the table as he spoke. Some of us leaned over to catch his words. "Nothing from that day except for...one bomber...a Fortress. Perhaps because...I had seen it...once before." For another minute he breathed, as if gathering air for his next words. "When I first saw the Fortress...two years ago...Herr Heydrich was on it."

I glanced at Hitler. I had heard Heydrich was one of his favorites, a veritable poster boy for National Socialism. But the *Führer* was drinking from his water glass.

"The next day," Schallhorn continued, "his car was...bombed."

Hitler put down his glass and shook his head. "He was a foolish man, I'm afraid, riding everywhere in that open Mercedes, giving partisans an easy target. So there was at least one American airplane without a half-naked woman on it?"

Some of the men chuckled. Schallhorn dipped his

head, held it that way for a moment, raised it again. "Perhaps I recall it because...before my crash...I saw it again."

"Are you sure it was the same one?" I asked.

He went on as if he had not heard. "This time I saw, quite clearly on its nose, three faces: a man, a woman...and a girl of about seven. This time it...startled me. I recognized them. They lived...in the house next to ours--"

"What happened to them?" I blurted it out, and immediately regretted it. Who said anything happened to them? But now I had the attention of all, Hitler included. I wanted to slide under the table.

Schallhorn went on, seemingly oblivious. "The man was a tailor...he belonged to the synagogue...in the center of town. At some point they wore...yellow stars. The plane even...showed them with...the stars. One day they...stopped coming home...we never knew...where they went."

"And you believe you saw them on a Yank bomber?" I pressed.

"Schallhorn," said Wiese. "Everything happens so fast in a battle. You think you saw them, but it was actually someone else. Probably dancing chorines?" Some of the men laughed.

Schallhorn shook his head, turning it right, then left, right, left. "No, I am afraid...not. It was more like...it saw me. I could only sit in my plane and...watch...until it released me. I could not have missed a...single detail. I wanted to...shoot it down."

I was staring down at my half-eaten lunch. "Schallhorn. That bomber...did you see its name? It was the Grim Reaper, wasn't it?"

All eyes were on me again. Schallhorn turned his head in his slow, careful way and, for the first time, made eye contact.

"Who did you see...Kellner?" he asked.

"I only saw the name. Glimpsed it."

This seemed to satisfy him. He returned his gaze to the tabletop. "Perhaps, Wiese...you are right. It may have been...dancing girls indeed, but...I remembered the first time, of course, when it was...Heydrich. And now seeing my neighbors there... But when I went down, I wondered why it was not...me. I realized, it must not have been...my time. So I knew I would live, whatever happened. Even if..." he forced a grin with lips that only partially covered his teeth, "I am not quite the same."

Hitler picked up a last forkful of spinach salad, holding it near his mouth as he spoke. "So it appears the Americans are even painting Jewish atrocity propaganda on their airplanes."

"Well, Schallhorn!" Krupinski broke in. "You really have made an astonishingly fast recovery. How did you do it?"

"Oh. Yes. You should see...the wonders...at the hospital."

"I did not need a war," Hitler said, "but since it was brought upon us, our men of science have risen to the occasion."

"Yes," Schallhorn agreed, but omitted the customary *my Führer* at the end. "The machines, they made a fright of buzzing, and dials spinning...and the clicking of gears or something inside them... And the hoses, and no end of cables sucking at me like lampreys...there were times I was feverish, I imagined them as actual animals feeding on me...a single piercing prick on each arm and my right leg, but a mass of them between my head and waist...sucking, sucking...I may have screamed once and they had to...calm me down...but in the end...got me through."

"And so you were able to join us here," Hartmann said. "And you have your Diamonds." He raised his coffee cup.

"Yes. It is only..." Schallhorn hesitated. "One doctor was too quick to tell me about...one of the wonder machines."

"We are producing wonder weapons," Hitler went on, "jets and rockets, blitz bombers that will drive the allies back to the channel, and repel the Bolshevik hordes back to Moscow--"

"The machine he spoke of," said Schallhorn, "made the difference...the doctors said. They had received it...only the day before, with the specialist who...spoke to me. He came from Buchenwald Camp. I asked him how they had...tested it. He said...'On volunteers.'"

"Major Kellner?" Hitler broke the silence. He must have seen something in my face. "Does this have some special meaning to you?"

"No, my *Führer*." I emphasized that last part.

But Schallhorn was talking again. "I had time to think...lying there. When the Allies crushed Hamburg...eight days and seven nights of...relentless bombing...people said it was because of what we had done...to the Jews."

I tensed, and now watched Hitler, along with all the others.

Schallhorn went on. "I heard that Minister Speer said...it put the fear of God into him. And...a curious thing...the immense air raid bunkers there, and in other cities...some were built...on the ruins of synagogues."

"Oh! Yes!" I tried a laugh, but it sputtered out. "That is simply these times, Schallhorn. You know how General Milch had to get a blood certificate, that his father wasn't actually his Jewish father, but an Uncle..."

I stopped, and again wanted to fall under the table. Two of the men were gaping at me now, and Hitler's eyes had caught fire.

"The Jews," Hitler in a low rasp, "are a parasitic race. It was Jewry, Kellner, that brought this war upon us! And the ones in America pulling Roosevelt's puppet strings, it is they who are sending these bombers day after day in their relentless intention to destroy us!" His voice was rising now to the voice the world knew, the Nuremburg Hitler, the one Hartmann had so comically mimicked earlier. No one laughed now. The other pilots kept blank faces or looked across the room. The waiters stood some distance off.

Still pinning me under his glare, Hitler stabbed a finger at Schallhorn. "Do you want to know what their vision is for us? Look at him!"

During this time. Krupinski fumbled in his pocket and brought out a cigarette case. Hitler disliked smoking as much as meat. Krupinski made a show of pulling one out, sticking it in his mouth and bringing up a lighter.

Hitler finally noticed. "Krupinski! That is a disgusting habit. You should think about quitting that."

He apologized, and hastened to put the cigarette case away. I shot him a look that said *Thank you.* He nodded.The rest of the meal passed quietly, and when it ended, we were dismissed.

III

Another morning, another alarm, another armada darkening our skies. The day was 19 July.

Feldwebel Beck had been shot down a week before. His accordion still lay on a table where he had left it. Of course I thought of that Fortress--had he appeared on it? Was it even flying that day, or was it on the ground being repaired? Did men's faces show on it even then, for the repair crews to wonder who they were? It might be a Russian Yak pilot, who had bailed out and whose parachute did not open. Or a British pilot, or the whole crew of a Lancaster or Halifax? Or, perhaps even a whole host of faces, a hundred of them covering the whole plane, German citizens suffocating in a shelter beneath the pounding bombs, the fires above them sucking away their oxygen?

I climbed into the icy air, wearing my Oak Leaves between my lapels.

Reaching altitude, we were confronted with truly an awe-inspiring sight. More than a thousand Fortresses, along with some two hundred fighters that included the long-range Mustangs. The twin-engined, fork-tailed Lightnings had also come. Opposing these were forty 109's and FW-190's. But if we were down to only two aircraft, we would still rise to meet them.

I forgot about hunting one particular bomber. It would be like trying to pick out a single falcon in a flock of hundreds, and while hornets are attacking you besides. It was the least of my concerns. But inside of a minute, I saw it--more like found myself confronted with it--that accursed GRIM REAPER, humming on the leading edge of that armada. Like they wanted us to see it, to remind us (as if a reminder was needed) what they intended for our homeland. As if seeking me out--why me?--my 109G with the blue-green camouflage, the number 22 on its fuselage, and 120 kills and Oak Leaves marked on its rudder.

And the bomber's nose bore a new face.

At that moment I flared with anger, my grip tightened on the stick, my muscles snapped taut, and I could think of nothing except I wanted that airplane.

Such was my thought that I forgot the standard head-on attack. I flew over and past the armada instead, bombers flashing by in silver blurs beneath me, one after another, hundreds in an instant. I cursed, kicking my crate right and swinging back around.

Catching back up with the formation's vanguard, the top turret gunners spitting bullets in twinkles of light, I sought the Reaper again, knowing I would have no trouble spotting it. I wanted to confirm I had really seen what I thought I saw. With what the whole world now knows, you've probably guessed who it was.

Could it all really be some trick of my mind? And Schallhorn's? War seems to weaken rationality and invite the most outlandish things for which we cannot account.

But there it was, no different from the other Fortresses except the infernal paint job on its nose, and yet, as I expected, my eyes found it.

It was not Hitler's first appearance on an airplane, of course. I had seen a cartoon on another Fortress called AROUND THE CORNER. It showed a hunter who looked like the Elmer Fudd character, holding a shotgun in one hand and Hitler's severed, bleeding head high in the other.

This time, however, they made the *Führer* himself cartoonish. He was clutching his head with both hands like the painting *The Cry*, as jagged yellow flashes of an explosion radiated out around him.

I peered through my canopy at the sight and thought: You son. Of. A. Bitch.

Whatever it took, I was going to bring that plane down.

Mustangs, Thunderbolts swarmed at me as if reading my thoughts. I hit my methanol emergency booster and turned and dived and looped and spun, trying to shake them while at the same time keeping the accursed Reaper in view. Now it was above me to the left, now below and to the right, now some distance aft as I kept up the dance with my opponents and machine guns spat their pearl necklace rounds. In spite of the cold air, I sweated. A tight turn wrenched me back in my seat, then I hung upside down in my safety harness with my guts coming up into my mouth. When a fighter flew across my gunsight I fired, and even got one Lightning's right engine to smoke. But I wanted to save my ammunition for the brute that spelled death for my leader.

Three Focke-Wulfs arrived and gave my opponents something else to worry about. Shaking off a Mustang, I swept around to the right and closed in on the Reaper's seven o'clock, pouring out rounds in one long burst. The tail and waist gunners responded, sparking out their streams of bullets. Only now do I wonder, who would crew such a plane? What do they have to do with its art? But I thought of none of this at the time, nor that I never seemed to see the waist gunners, who stand in open windows. I thought only that *I wanted that plane.*

But it wasn't going down. I fired my 20mm through my propeller, fired again. The bomber's guns blazed on as I weaved closer. Bullets struck my fuselage, *woomf-woomf,* and another *woomf* shook my port wing. I glimpsed bits of the wing flying off, but I jammed the throttle forward, sweat streaming down my face. I threw my last 20mm round at that beast. Nothing at all existed now except for the Fortress growing bigger and bigger in my vision. Its waist guns, tail guns hammered but I was too close now, the huge rudder rushing up. I watched it calmly in the final few seconds, time hanging still, and fully expected my life to end now instead of Hitler's.

I hit home with a shriek of metal shearing through metal. A flurry of shards flew. My crate shuddered as if it had slammed into a wall, but it kept going, slicing through the rudder and across the top of the fuselage. My propeller stopped spinning, grotesquely bent, and the whole front was crumpled. Descending fast, the cockpit smelling of glycol, I fought to keep the wings level.

Where? I looked all around. *Where is he?*

There. Far off to my right, the Fortress was descending faster than I was. I had left a ragged gap in the front of its rudder, and the port elevator had torn off entirely. The letters GRIM REAPER glared scarlet on its nose as if in defiance, seeming to illuminate my last sight of cartoon-Hitler as it spiraled downward, trailing no smoke.

Flames licked from my wrecked engine now. I jettisoned the canopy, unfastened the safety belt, and forced the stick to one side. The plane rolled, and I fell clear. After a few moments I pulled the ripcord. The parachute blossomed overhead and caught me with a jerk.

I watched the Fortress's descent all the way down. No crewmen bailed out, no parachutes. It struck a meadow with a blast of its entire bomb load detonating, the flame mushrooming up yellow and red. Black smoke climbed into the sky.

IV

And that completes my account.

By now, the whole world knows of the assassination attempt at Hitler's Rastenburg headquarters. It took place the next day. Not poison or a gunshot, but an attempt to explode him out of life like the Fortresses, Liberators, and Lancasters blasting Germany, little by little, out of existence. It is telling, I think, that this was the method used. Unlike Germany, however, Hitler was spared and the Fortress killed instead. It *crashed*. It was as if the Reaper was able to penetrate our skies and so begin its task, but brought down before it could complete it.

It was the explosion at Rastenburg, however, that reverberated through the country. It sent Hitler insane with rage and paranoia; sweeping arrests soon followed. Schallhorn, I am to understand, had some sort of hand in the plot. By now he has been executed. And I wait, alone in this cell, for my turn to be shot. Sleeping in here last night, the lights did not go out but instead glared brighter. The Gestapo evidently meant to deny me even my last night of sleep.

Why? Perhaps Schallhorn named me. Perhaps it was some remark I made over lunch that day, or that Hitler thought I made. I can only guess, just as I can only guess why only Schallhorn, and then myself, ever saw that plane's devilry. Perhaps others had as well. But evil--most of the time--seems to happen in such a random, chance manner. Most likely, it happened for no reason at all.

And Hitler will never know I saved his life.

Article

The Lazzaretto And The Ghost Child.
Viviana De Cecco

The Lazzaretto of Sant'Elia is a place of peace and silence, surrounded by a small park and a long pier overlooking the sea of Cagliari, the capital of the Italian island of Sardinia, where the transparency of the water changes from emerald green to deep blue. Many people come here to take a walk, walk their dogs, ride their bikes, or have lunch at the nearby restaurant to taste local specialties. In the distance you can also see the timeless silhouette of the Sant'Elia Tower, which stands guard over the promontory that frames the coastal landscape. Silence pervades the landscape, a few ships stand out on the calm horizon as they make their way to the city's port, and three Spanish cannons recall the historic battles of past centuries when the Sardinian people tried to protect their land from foreign invasion.

Sardinia has always been a wild place, full of myths and legends, where ghosts have inhabited hundreds of places that are part of our daily lives. I, too, have been visiting the Lazzaretto for years, which has recently become a cultural center where art and photography exhibitions, open-air concerts and book presentations take place. It seems strange to think that this place, surrounded by such a serene atmosphere, was once a place of death and now bears traces of mysterious apparitions.

I have always had a special interest in haunted places, because I like to believe that not only objects, stones or buildings can represent traces of human existence, but also the intangible manifestations of what we call the soul. The Lazaretto is a place where one can gather concrete clues to what can only be perceived through the senses. Since I collaborate with the Italian website "La Soglia Oscura", where parapsychologists, writers and ordinary people provide testimonies of paranormal events, I decided to interview the director of the Lazaretto to find out if the rumors circulating in the city about the child ghost have any basis.

Entering through an imposing entrance arch on the street side, one reaches a grassy path that leads to the entrance of the museum. In the center of the square building there is a large courtyard where you can admire an ancient Roman anchor recovered from the seabed and an underground cistern that peeks through the ground and was used to store water, now covered by an ornate iron grate. This grate is the only way to peer into the dark depths of the ground. But it is in the long interior corridors, spread over two floors, that a rather lively and sometimes mischievous ghost seems to roam.

The legend began in the 1970s, when the Lazzaretto was an abandoned building overgrown with weeds. One summer evening, some twelve-year-old kids from the nearby neighborhood decided to take refuge in the dilapidated building to smoke cigarettes in secret, away from their parents' eyes. There were four of them, and none of them had ever believed in ghosts.

They crossed the threshold with typical adolescent bravado, thinking they were safe from prying eyes. At first, nothing happened. The four sat in the courtyard on the old, rickety steps of the outside staircase leading to the second floor and smoked quietly.

Suddenly, as the moonlight shone in the sky above their heads, one of them felt a cold draft. It was August, and the night temperature was near 35 degrees. The boy tensed up, but tried not to pay much attention to the strange occurrence.

A short time later, however, another boy rubbed his hands as if he were cold. Eventually, the other two confessed to feeling something unusual as well. At that moment, while they were cautiously looking around, they heard a faint whisper coming from the back of the courtyard. It sounded like a child's high-pitched voice. They turned abruptly, and it's said that they all saw a shadow no more than a foot tall move quickly along the walls. From that day on, after the incident was shared with other friends and relatives, the legend began to circulate beyond the neighborhood streets and spread like wildfire among young and old throughout the city.

In the historical archives of the province and hospitals there are hundreds of names of children who died in the Lazaretto, so it would have been impossible to discover the name of this child-voiced ghost. Since then, he has simply been called the Ghost Child.

There is no sadder death than that of a child snatched from life by fate and a terrible disease that has claimed thousands of victims in past centuries, both in Sardinia and in the rest of Italy. The poignant first-hand testimony of Morgan, director of the Cagliari Lazaretto, evokes a shiver of fear and, at the same time, a feeling of pity for the poor soul of the young ghost that seems to move up and down the solid walls of what was, between the 1600s and 1800s, a shelter for victims of plague, smallpox and typhus.

It appears that it was petechial or hemorrhagic typhus (so named because of the punctual bleeding caused by a bacterium transmitted by lice) that tragically took the life of this child, who was about seven years old. Born and raised in the Sant'Elia neighborhood, Morgan has worked at the Lazaretto for twenty-two years. With his calm voice, which reflects a sense of compassion for all those who have been confined to this place of suffering in the past centuries, he recounted the paranormal experiences that he had not only witnessed firsthand, but that had also happened to a lady from Cagliari who visited the center.

"A few years ago," he begins, "a lady who had enrolled in one of the art courses offered at the Lazaretto felt the presence of a supernatural being around her. Endowed with extraordinary sensitivity, she was able to recognize that it was a child of about seven years old. With my help, she asked me to conduct an experiment to see if her feelings were confirmed. We took a ball and put it in a room in the museum and left it there overnight. The next day, when we went to check on its whereabouts, we found that it had been moved to a completely different room than where we had left it. Surprised by the result of this test, we tried to communicate with the being. Sensing other perceptions, like a whisper in the silence, the lady asked us to plant yellow flowers in a beautiful flower bed in the center of the courtyard, as she had the impression that the child was somehow pleasantly attracted to them. Perhaps the poor child had retained memories of pleasant outdoor walks during his childhood," Morgan explains.

It is not hard to imagine the anguish of a child wandering alone in the silence and darkness of those dimly lit corridors, where Morgan himself had a disturbing experience. "My colleagues and I were charged with putting together an exhibition of pre-Columbian art. Since the legend of the child ghost had been circulating in Cagliari for some time, I thought we could attract tourists with something more interesting than a mere exhibition. But my colleague disagreed. He thought it was inappropriate and wrong to disturb the dead. I replied, "If the dead were unhappy with this initiative, I think they would have let us know. At that moment we were in one of the galleries on the upper floor, with twenty-two lights that could only be turned on by twenty-two switches arranged on a single electrical panel. But as soon as I finished saying these words, all the lights went on simultaneously, as if someone had pressed all twenty-two buttons on the panel at the same time. Frightened and shaken by this inexplicable event, we took refuge outside, and my colleague finished his night shift in the car!"

"And you're still here?" I ask in surprise. "I would have run away immediately! Aren't you afraid? What do the visitors think?"

"No, we realized that this ghost doesn't want to hurt us. Either it's lonely or it just wants to have some fun. Visitors are usually fascinated by these phenomena. Many of them are skeptical.

"Have there been any other occurrences since that day?"

Morgan nods solemnly. After that disturbing experience, he and his colleague continued to feel the presence of the little ghost. "Once, when we had to set up an exhibition on the ancient costumes of Sardinia, we had taken mannequins and placed them along the walls of the main hall to show clothing from the late nineteenth century.

The next morning, however, we found the mannequins' heads detached. They had rolled on the floor. We even found the lace collar of a woman's dress torn. When we put it on the mannequin, it was perfectly intact. It had been donated by the descendants of one of the city's noble families and belonged to a woman with dark hair and a very sweet face. To highlight the story of the dress, we had placed an old photograph of the owner, given to us by her great-granddaughter. We thought that the woman might remind the child of his or her mother or grandmother.

Or maybe a woman who had been with him in the hospital and had taken him under her wing to comfort him during his terrible illness. And then..." Morgan paused and instinctively looked up, where the second-floor windows were visible.

"Were there any other incidents?" I urged him to continue.

"During a comic book exhibition, a Donald Duck comic was repeatedly found to be out of place, especially on a table where visitors were free to browse illustrated comic books or modern graphic novels. My colleague on duty would put it back on the shelf in perfect alignment with the other issues, but as soon as he turned his back, he would find it back on the table. Moreover, in the music room, where there was an exhibition of Launeddas, the ancient wind instruments of the island, the apparition seemed to play them, producing a long whistle that echoed through the deserted rooms. At times, a lady thought she saw the child's shadow behind the glass of some windows overlooking an old catwalk used for a "modeling posture" class.

Finally, Morgan explained that even a local paranormal team had spent several nights in the building, hoping to gather tangible evidence of these mysterious presences. Sadly, no anomalies were found.

Although there is no scientific proof of the events that took place, it is safe to assume that the spirits made their opinions known in a rather dramatic manner. It is easy to imagine the terror experienced by Morgan and his colleague in those brief moments when, in the darkness of the night, that immense glow convinced them that it was never wise to disturb the dead, torn from life by the brutality of a violent and sudden death.

Even today, many people claim to have heard voices coming from the deserted corridors when darkness falls and only the moonlight illuminates the Lazaretto. Are these really the souls of the poor dead, reminding the living of the suffering and loneliness they endured, isolated from the outside world and plagued by unimaginable tortures? Today, it is said that some night watchmen have seen the child ghost playing ball with a skull, in a more macabre version than the one provided by Morgan. Some even claim that the elevator often gets stuck between floors, as if some presence wants to prevent visitors from ascending to the silent great halls and disturbing it. That's why it's better to take the stairs when visiting the Lazaretto. That is, if you don't happen to see a child's ball rolling down the stairs. Or a skull, who knows...

Article

Trilogy of Terror: The Horror of Female Archetypes Explored and Reversed
Denise Noe

A made-for-TV movie, *Trilogy of Terror* first aired on March 4, 1975 and instantly rocketed to cult status – a status that has grown in the decades since its initial broadcast. As an Internet Movie Database "User Reviewer" noted, "It continues to gain new fans each and every year." *Complex* magazine ranked it ***4 on a list of scariest TV movies of all time and MeTV lauded it as *the* scariest TV movie.

As the title suggests, *Trilogy* consists of three separate episodes. Each segment is based on a short story by acclaimed horror writer Richard Matheson. The first two screenplays were penned by William F. Nolan while Matheson himself wrote the screenplay for the final episode. Each segment stars Karen Black and she plays four different parts. It was directed by Dan Curtis, director of such TV horror classics as the soap opera *Dark Shadows* and another famous made-for-TV movie, *The Night Stalker*.

This essay will examine the qualities that turned *Trilogy* into a cult film and argue that a major reason for its special status is often overlooked.

Three Segments Summarized

The first segment is "Julie" and opens on a university campus. Two lusty young college students, Chad (Robert Burton, Karen Black's then-husband) and Eddie (James Storm) are checking out the young coeds as they pass by. Chad comments on what "dogs" the young women are and Eddie calls Chad "spoiled." A bespectacled woman garbed modestly in drab beige clothes, her brown hair in a loose bun and her arms piled high with books, walks by. "Now that's ugly!" Eddie exclaims. But Chad seems disconcerted. "I wonder what she looks like under all those clothes," he admits. Eddie seems perplexed that a fellow male student could possible find Professor Julie Eldridge (Karen Black) alluring. Chad comments, "It's kind of like the idea just jumped into my head."

Conveniently enough, Chad is taking an English class with Professor Eldridge. As the teacher talks, she sits on her desk. Her long, dull beige skirt rides up and Chad gets a welcome eyeful of shapely leg. He fantasizes about her lying on a bed. When class is dismissed, Chad follows her outside. As when first seen, Julie is carrying a large stack of books. A book drops on the floor so Chad chivalrously picks it up and hands to her. He tells her he likes to go to movies. He adds that he tends to think in pictures so his hobby is, appropriately enough, photography. They part as she tells him she must be going and heads elsewhere.

That evening, Julie Eldridge is correcting papers when her friend Anne (Kathryn Reynolds) remonstrates with the prof about her all-work-and-no-play lifestyle. Anne tries to get Julie to consider a blind date but Julie is not interested. Anne expresses dismay at her friend's dowdy appearance, assuring Julie that she "could really be attractive" if she would just work at it. Julie indicates that she is satisfied with focusing on her career. As soon as Anne exists, we see that visually minded Chad is skulking in the bushes around Julie's residence. He peeks in a window and watches as she frees her long hair from its bun to slowly brush it and then peels off her clothes.

The next day, Chad chats with the professor after a class. He asks her to a "wonderful old vampire movie" that is a "real classic." He adds that the movie is "all in French with English subtitles" and suggests they see it "for reasons of cultural expansion."

Julie tells him she is flattered by his interest but adds that the rules of the college forbid teachers and students from dating. Additionally, she expresses confusion at his interest: "You have your pick of all these lovely coeds, Chad. Why would you want to date me?"

"I admire maturity in a woman," he answers. Chad appears to be a determined man-on-the-make as he pursues this solitary, shy professor.

Julie agrees to the date.

They go to a theater and watch a vampire film. There is a wry in-joke because the film seen briefly on the screen is no French classic requiring English subtitles but Dan Curtis's 1972 TV movie *The Night Stalker*. Chad asks if Julie would like a beverage. She would. After sipping the soft drink, she observes, "It's bitter."

Of course, it is bitter because the nefarious Chad slipped something into the drink. It works: she loses consciousness. Chad heads for a motel where he cheekily registers himself and his date as "Mr. and Mrs. Jonathan Harker." In the room, he rapes her and takes numerous photographs of her lying on the bed.

At the end of their date, Julie realizes she fell asleep during the film and apologizes for being poor company. Chad, in his turn, apologizes for taking her to a boring film. He tells her he would like another date but she retorts that there will be no more dates as it was foolish for them to have even had one.

There is a brief scene of Chad developing photos followed by a ringing telephone awakening Julie from slumber. Chad demands Julie meet with him. When she does, he shows her the sexually compromising photographs he took of her. "My hobby is photography," he reminds her. "You drugged me!" she realizes. He readily admits it. She threatens to report him to the police. He retorts that she has no proof she was drugged. If she brings the police into it, he will tell them that she initiated their relationship and has a "thing" for students, offering the incriminating pics as proof.

"What do you want from me?" she asks.

His silent leer tells what he wants: she must serve his sexual desires or face professional ruin and public disgrace.

When another class is in session, Chad hands Julie a note saying there are friends at his place that he wants her to meet. She soon dismisses the class.

The next scene shows Julie returning home. Apparently, she is currently sharing her place with Anne who demands to know what is going on. Julie refuses to give any satisfactory answer. She appears depressed – as would be expected. We have been given to believe that this poor woman has just been blackmailed into being sexually passed around among a group of young men.

The next scene shows Chad and Julie together in a room. Julie hands Chad a drink which he happily gulps.

"It's over, Chad," she crisply informs him.

"Nothing is over until I say it is," he replies.

Julie gives him a knowing, superior smile and tells him that she is bored. And when she is bored, the game is over.

"Bored?" he inquires in confusion.

"Not shocked, not terrified, just plain bored," she says. "Whose idea did you think this whole thing was anyway?" She informs Chad that it was not his "dull little mind" that originated the "rather dramatic experiences we've shared." She rhetorically asks, "Why do you think you suddenly had the desire to see what I looked like 'under all those clothes'? Since that moment, your mind has not been your own." She tells him not to feel bad as she always gets bored after a brief period, adding, "Although there was one young man who kept me amused for almost nine weeks – but then he was wonderfully creative."

Chad is obviously flummoxed at the realization that

Julie has implanted thoughts into his mind. He has just learned that he is not the rapist but the raped. Through her witchlike control of his mind, he has been enacting Julie's sexual fantasies, not his.

The shocked, flustered Chad begins violently gagging. Julie coolly informs him that he will soon experience cardiac arrest. He accuses her of drugging him and she corrects, "No, dear, I've killed you." He falls down dead. Julie drags his corpse into his amateur photographer's darkroom. She finds the negatives of the sexy pictures he took of her and lights them on fire.

In the next scene, Julie is sniffling softly and reading a newspaper article about Chad's death. Anne comments that she must be very sad that one of her best students was just killed in such a horrifying accident. Does Julie need Anne to stay there to provide comfort? Julie assures Anne she can leave.

Once alone, Julie cuts out the article. Then she opens up a scrapbook containing articles about the mysterious deaths of various young men – obviously her previous victims. Julie is both witch (understood as someone with supernatural powers rather than follower of the Wicca religion) and serial murderer. The modest, prim English professor makes a habit of invading the minds of young men, having them enact her sexual fantasies, and murdering them when she loses interest.

The doorbell rings. Arthur Moore (Gregory Harrison) would like help. "My lit grades are lousy," he said. Would Professor Eldridge have time for tutoring?

"Of course, I do," she says with a warm smile. As she closes the door behind them, she adds, "I think we're going to be friends, Arthur -- very good friends."

"Millicent and Therese" is about a good sister and a bad sister. Our initial encounter is with good sister Millicent who we see operating a projector showing home movies. The home movie displays a classic wholesome family scene of a mommy, daddy, big fluffy dog, and girl of about twelve. The girl runs happily into the arms of her loving father. He picks her up in his arms and spins her around.

It seems like a heartwarming aw' shucks family scene but Millicent's expression is grim. Like Julie, Millicent is bespectacled and bun-wearing although the appearance is different as Millicent's glasses are wire-rimmed while Julie's were horn-rimmed and Millicent's bun is tight while Julie's was loose. Like Julie, Millicent dresses modestly and drably but while Julie is given to beige and brown, Millicent is given to black dresses with lace around the collar. The characters may share similarities but they are distinct.

After watching the home movie, Millicent sits at a desk and pens into a journal that the funeral is over and she is alone in the house but "Therese is out cavorting with one of her men on this night when father is barely cold in his casket." She continues that she ran the old family films to remind herself about her sister and how "even at twelve she was already using her wiles on him." Millicent goes on to mourn the thought of "poor mother" could "never suspect the depth of evil in Therese." Millicent continues that she was never fooled by Therese's "sweet little face" but saw "the fermenting ugliness in her soul."

Cut to a scene in which Millie opens the front door. She invites the visitor, Mr. Anmar (John Karlen), inside. She immediately tells him that she knows what he must be wondering: how can sisters look so different? "I have never found it necessary to affect the ways of Therese," Millicent explains. She tells Anmar that Therese had gone to a party. He is perplexed since he knows her father's funeral was on that very day. "My sister is an unusual girl. I doubt that you truly understand her – which is why I've called you here." She shows the visitor an old family photo of Therese and their father. She says, "I want you to notice the way she's pressing herself against him." Anmar expresses bewilderment about what she is trying to tell him. Millicent elaborates that her sister is evil and was evil from childhood. "But father worshipped her and she him," Millicent states. "When she was sixteen, she seduced him." Anmar appears offended and says he does not wish to hear more. Despite his offense, Millicent continues that soon after the incest began, "Mother died.

The doctors said it was an accident, that she had taken an overdose of sleeping pills. But it was no accident – it was Therese." Anmar asks why Millicent stayed in the same house with her wicked sister and Millicent answers that she had no money or way or earning any so she just kept to herself and tried to ignore Therese.

Again, Anmar seems bewildered. Millie goes to the bookcase and points out the books Therese collects on demonology, pornography, Satanism, voodoo, and witchcraft. Millie says Therese is guided by Satan and her soul is damned. "I cannot help her," Millie says in a tone of desperation, her eyes glistening with tears. "But I can help you."

"Miss Larrimore, I'm afraid you're the one who really needs help," Anmar replies in evident exasperation.

Millicent lets out a bitter laugh. She tells Anmar that Therese does not really care for him but lies to him and laughs at him.

Clearly fed up with Millicent's stream of accusations at the woman he believes loves him, he tells her he is going and turns on his heel.

"I know all about that night in Morley and what happened there," Millicent exclaims.

Anmar stops in his tracks. He clearly did not expect his girlfriend to describe certain details of their intimacies to her sister. Then Millicent lets him know that Therese "gloated" and "bragged" about how "she was able to corrupt" him. Ahhhhh . . . just what type of "corruption" was this? "My sister enjoys inflicting pain Mr. Anmar and somehow she somehow persuaded you to share in this perversion," Millicent asserts.

Anmar looks devastated with shame. He now believes Therese is evil. "Then you are saved, Mr. Anmar," Millicent says with evident satisfaction. "I have freed you from evil."

It should be remembered that, in 1975, much of middle-class America still used "perversion" to describe BDSM activities so the mention of a night of consensually inflicted pain lent a powerful aura of dark decadence to *Trilogy*.

The next scene shows our heroine again writing in her

journal. Apparently, Therese was none-too-pleased about that Millicent "dared to reveal the truth to Mr. Anmar" so an infuriated Therese messed up Millicent's room and raged and swore at her. Millicent complains that Therese is becoming worse, adding, "It's as if father's death has released the demons within her and I actually fear for my life."

The next conversation occurs over the phone between Millicent and Dr. Chester Ramsey (George Gaynes). The distressed Millicent complains that Therese's behavior has become "much worse" and that she has even suggested that the relationship between Millicent and Dr. Ramsey is one that is "lewd" and "sordid."

The physician states that he will be in the area tomorrow. When he is, he will visit Millicent to discuss her troubles with her sister. When we see the doctor at the Larrimore home, we also see his smile dry up when the door is opened by a heavily made-up woman with long blonde hair. Her bright orange miniskirt and platform shoes are quite a contrast to Millicent's attire.

Therese invites the doctor in and let him know that she is aware of what Millicent told Ramsey the previous day in their phone conversation because Therese listened in from the extension in her room. Then Therese told him it is apt to be a wasted visit, "Because I know Millicent won't talk about me when I'm in the house – and here I am."

He asks about her vandalizing Millicent's room. Therese readily admits to it. "Where does that little twit get off thinking she's got the right to stick her nose into my affairs?" she rhetorically asks before lighting a cigarette.

"Therese, this hatred has got to stop," Dr. Ramsey cautions. "You'll destroy yourself."

The doctor's words make no impression on Therese who soon becomes blatantly seductive. Dr. Ramsey shows no sexual interest in her. He gets up to leave and she taunts him, asking if the gray-haired man is "still a virgin." When he is at the door, Therese bitterly yells at him, "We don't need you anymore, Ramsey! Why don't you just get the hell out of lives! Don't phone and don't call on us!"

Then Therese goes to the door of her sister's room where she pounds the door and yells at Millicent that Dr. Ramsey is gone and unlikely to be back.

In the next scene, Therese is writing in her journal about the incident and how she cannot stand to "watch evil prevail," concluding the only solution is that "Therese must die."

The next scene shows a little girl outside the Larrimore home, holding a doll and crying. Millicent sees her and rushes to the child. "My dolly is broken," the child says, "Your sister broke it." The child recounts an incident in which Therese accused the girl of making too much noise and broke her cherished toy. "I hate her, Miss Millicent, I hate her!" the child chokes out between sobs. Millicent comforts the child and promises to buy her a new doll.

The broken doll inspires Millicent to realize "the solution" to the Therese problem. Millicent will murder Therese – not in the usual manner but using "Therese's own weapons against her" by killing her through voodoo. She takes clippings from her sister's long fingernails left in an ashtray, strands of her blonde hair left in a hairbrush, and rhinestone buttons "from her most lewdly seductive dress."

Millicent phones Dr. Ramsey and cheerfully tells him that "things are different now" and she has "found a way to deal with Therese." He demands to see her and talk but she says that is unnecessary and the conversation ends. We see Millicent pull from a desk drawer a voodoo doll and pick up a long pin.

An alarmed Dr. Ramsey heads to the Larrimore home. The front door is open and he goes inside calling, "Millicent! Millie, are you here?" He searches through the house and finds Therese dead on the floor, the voodoo doll beside her corpse. Dr. Ramsey calls for an ambulance. After the ambulance arrives, he talks to the attendants. He explains that he was the family physician. He kneels beside the dead woman. He wipes the bright red lipstick off and pulls the blonde wig off. He says, "Her name was

Therese Millicent Larrimore – the most advanced case of dual personality I have ever encountered."

The third story is "Amelia." It opens with Amelia carrying a large package into her apartment. She has a less extreme look than any previous Black character in the film. She lacks the blatant sexuality of Therese but does not have the hangdog modesty of Julie or Millicent. Rather, she seems to be a rather typical 1970s young lady. She lives in a high-rise and we watch her travel up the elevator to her apartment. There she opens the package. It contains a "Zuni hunting fetish," a spear-carrying doll with dramatically sharply pointed teeth and a face sculpted into a fierce grimace. The scroll that comes with the doll labels it "He Who Kills." Amelia smiles at the doll and marvels, "Why, are you ugly!" Then she adds, "Even your mother wouldn't love you." She taps the end of the doll's spear and notes its sharpness. "Arthur's going to love it," she comments. Then she calls her mother. We only hear Amelia's side of the conversation but it is obvious that her mother is domineering and controlling. We learn that Amelia purchased the doll for her beau, a professor of anthropology. The doll supposedly has a Zuni hunter's spirit inside it and the thin gold chain about the doll keeps that spirit from coming to life. The conversation goes from the doll to how Amelia will spend that evening. This is a day that mother and daughter usually visit but she tells Mom she wants to spend the evening with her boyfriend because it is his birthday. As the conversation continues, the tension in Amelia's voice rises as it becomes evident that she resents her mother's domination but cannot free of it. Mom appears to be an expert manipulator who makes her daughter feel guilty for no longer living with her mother and for even dating at all. In a pained voice, Amelia denies that she breaks promises to Mom. "Please stop treating me like a child!" Amelia exclaims. "I'm grown up!" Amelia appears close to tears.

When Mom hangs up the phone, Amelia looks at the doll and tells it that she is going to take a bath and then see her "fella." She bangs the doll down on the table and – wouldn't you know it? – that gold chain that is supposed to keep the killer's spirit from coming to life falls off with a little clank.

We next see Amelia, in a bathrobe, making a phone call. It is to Arthur. She tells him she cannot keep their date. She has to give that evening to her mother because Mom was so upset that she even left home to live in her own place. She cannot hurt her mother's feelings.

Amelia heads to the kitchen to prepare the meal that she will later share with Mom. After starting the dinner, she returns to the living room. The doll is nowhere in sight. Hmmmm . . . what could have happened to it? Falling to her hands and knees, she stretches an arm beneath a couch and *ouch!* feels the sharp point of a little spear. Puzzled, she pulls out the spear – but no doll.

There is noise like the patter of little feet. "Is that you, little man?" she asks, laughing at the absurdity of the thought.

Something crashes in the kitchen. Amelia goes to investigate. The knife she had used to cut meat is nowhere in sight. She goes through the drawers and cannot find it. A small shadow dashes toward the living room and she goes there. A lamp's light goes out. She tries to turn it back on and realizes the Zuni doll is attacking her legs with her kitchen knife! She tries to run but the doll jumps on her, slashing brutally at her hands and arms. The bloodied and terrified Amelia races to her bedroom, slams the door behind her, and picks up the phone to call police.

She sees the doorknob start to turn. The doll is in the room and climbs atop Amelia's bed as she runs to the bathroom. The doll jabs the knife under the door. "This can't be happening!" Amelia shrieks.

The doll gets into the bathroom. In desperation, Amelia grabs a towel and wraps it around the doll. Then she puts the cloth-covered tiny monster into the bathtub water. She cannot drown it. Amelia flees from the bathroom to a closet. She tries to hold that closet door shut but the doll is able to pull it open. Amelia holds a suitcase open and the doll runs into it. She slams the suitcase shut, seemingly trapping the little monster. She takes the suitcase to the kitchen where he ever-determined demon-doll uses the kitchen knife to cut through the suitcase. In her panic, Amelia tries to grab the knife by its sharp and gets badly cut. The doll is almost out of the suitcase when Amelia fiercely attacks it with a screwdriver. The doll does not give any evidence of movement. Amelia seems to think she has killed it and opens up the suitcase whereupon the doll sinks its teeth into her arm. Amelia swings the doll against furniture and runs into the kitchen. The doll sinks its teeth into her neck.

A shrieking Amelia pulls open the door of the oven in which dinner is burning and throws the doll in whereupon everything in the oven goes up in flames! A cloud of black smoke roars out of the oven. When things appear to die down, she opens the oven door only to see more fire and lets out a piercing scream.

Cut to a scene in which Amelia, seemingly recovered and oddly calm after such a shocking ordeal, phones her mother. She apologizes for having been difficult and adds, "I think we should spend the evening together, just the way we planned." She ends the call saying, "I'll be waiting for you."

Amelia pulls the latch from the apartment door. She crouches before the door, a huge butcher knife in her hand, her teeth transformed into jagged and sharpened images like the teeth of the doll. It appears the spirit of the murderous Zuni fetish doll now possesses her.

The Cult Status of *Trilogy*

What explains the cult status of this made-for-TV movie? The film certainly benefits from the brilliance of its source material since all three segments are inspired by short stories penned by Richard Matheson. Born in 1926, the supremely talented Matheson became a published writer as a child when the *Brooklyn Eagle* published his poems and short stories. In 1950, his short story, "Born of Man and Woman," ran in *The Magazine of Fantasy and Science Fiction*. His novels include *I Am Legend* (1954) that is widely regarded as a science fiction classic and *The*

Incredible Shrinking Man that was adapted into a motion picture of the same name in 1957.

The director, Dan Curtis, was certainly another major plus. A producer and writer as well as a director, he is remembered for directing such acclaimed TV mini-series as *War and Remembrance* (1988-1989) and *The Winds of War* (1983) as well as such TV horror classics as the soap opera *Dark Shadows* and *The Night Stalker* (1972) and the series of the same title that came from it.

Some critics believe the special qualities of its star, Karen Black, catapulted *Trilogy* to cult status. A lovely woman, her look had a certain delightfully odd quality because her eyes were slightly crossed. The richly talented Black had already shot to fame with a performance in *Easy Rider* (1969). She garnered an Academy Award nomination for her performance in *Five Easy Pieces* (1970). Further acclaim was brought her way through her acting in *Nashville* (1975) and *Day of the Locust* (1975). Critic Gary Giddins praised her as "arguably the most inventive actress in 1970s Hollywood." Critic Jeremiah Kipp calls *Trilogy* "the Karen Black Show." He praises Black as "the kind of extreme actress who not only acts with her eyes and face, but with her neck, her fingertips, her elbows, wrists, and torso." At *The Loft Cinema*, a critic comments, "*Trilogy of Terror* gave the quirky Oscar-nominated actress the golden opportunity to put the acting pedal to the metal." A "user reviewer" on the Internet Movie Database (IMDb) comments that Black's "acting certainly helps make *Trilogy of Terror* so memorable." The same reviewer elaborates, "Black is certainly the main key here because she plays four different types of characters and does justice to them all."

Much of *Trilogy*'s cult status has been attributed specifically to its final segment. The technical wizardry behind the activities of the doll and the robustly terrifying chase it gave Amelia tend to stick in the minds of viewers. Black herself has suggested that the scene plays upon a primal, and specifically female, fear: "Women are afraid of vaginal entry." Giddins amplifies this observation: "especially by snakes, rats, and other small things like

Zuni fetish dolls." *The Loft Cinema* writer calls the Amelia segment "simultaneously hilarious and terrifying" and "pure kitschy gold." Jeremiah Kipp comments that people who see *Trilogy* "usually discuss this third episode exclusively, as well as the shock ending with Black's nefarious ear-to-ear grin."

The Horror of Female Archetypes Exposed and Reversed

It is this writer's belief that an overlooked factor underlying the special status of *Trilogy* is that all three segments explore horrors inherent in female sexual archetypes – and the realities that created those archetypes.

Much of the horror of "Julie" is based on the way expectations of gender are both reversed and subtly examined. Of course, the most obvious and dramatic reversal is that of victim and victimizer. In sex crimes, we expect – for good reason as it is usually this way in real life – that the male is the offender and the female the victim. This horror story turns this expectation upside down. An IMDb "user reviewer" considers this segment the "weakest link" because the surprise is "entirely untelegraphed" so it "feels like a cheap trick." I argue that, although the twist is certainly surprising, there have been clues to it. There is a hint that something more than meets eye and ear is going on when Chad wonders about the prof naked and adds, "It's kind of like the idea just jumped into my head."

There are also other, subtler, ways in which "Julie" telegraphs that there is something going on beneath the surface. Indeed, "Julie" explores the sexual games on multiple levels. For one thing, Professor Julie Eldridge is a sexual adventurer – indeed, a sexual predator – who has adopted a deliberately modest, even mousy, appearance. One of the ironies of modesty is that it can be its own kind of "sexy." In Wendy Shalit's *Modesty: Rediscovering the Lost Virtue*, she features a photograph from a nude beach captioned "nude and bored" contrasting with a photograph taken of the beachgoers in the early 20th Century caption "modest and mischievous." A woman who covers up may carry an aura of the "forbidden" about her that piques sexual interest. The fact that most of the body is covered can make it enticing when an exposure – however accidental or apparently accidental – occurs. Thus, a modestly attired woman whose long skirt rides up to expose her leg, as occurs with Julie, may be more enticing to at least some people than the mini-skirted woman. A bun is associated with an old-fashioned prudery but it has its own "tease" as it seems to invite the viewer to think about what it would be like to take that hair down. Another common part of the sexual game can be female feigned helplessness. The viewer may wonder if Julie's skirt riding up was entirely unintended. It may also be that her dropping a book close to Chad was not a true accident either.

Indeed, the horror of "Julie," in this writer's opinion, grows from the fusion of its subtle exploration of the sexuality of modesty and its dramatic reversal of our expectations about gender and sexual victimization. The next two segments of *Trilogy* both excavate and expose horror that can underlay parent-child relationships and, in particular, parent-daughter relationships.

An interesting aspect of "Millicent and Therese" is that it does not depend on the supernatural for its horror. It is *possible* that supernatural forces produced the death of the mentally ill woman but it is also possible that she died because she *believed* in the powers of witchcraft/voodoo.

"Millicent and Therese" is about the horror that can result from a twisted father-daughter relationship. Most of the public is familiar with a disorder that used to be classified as "Multiple Personality Disorder" through books/films like *The Three Faces of Eve* and *Sybil*. This disorder has been recategorized as "Dissociative Identity Disorder" – and for good reason. The terms by which it was formerly known were misleading and even tended to somewhat glamorize the illness. Multiple Personality suggests more than one personality in the same body. However, the disorder is not one of multiplied personalities but a single personality that has become so fractured that parts of the personality fail to recognize itself.

The story of "Millicent and Therese" symbolizes that fracturing and how it can occur. Although Millicent speaks disdainfully of a 16-year-old Therese as "seducing" her father, decent people generally agree that the adult (male or female) is responsible in an inappropriate relationship between said adult and a minor. And indeed, that home movie in which Millicent sees Therese as "using her wiles" only shows a child hugging her father as any child might.

The true horror of this story is that Therese Millicent Larrimore's father molested and raped her. The adult betrayed his true parental role but the child, confused and violated, blamed herself. The trauma of sexual abuse, and the crushing sense of shame and guilt associated with it, caused the child's personality to fracture. As an adult, she found herself unable to bear the self-alienation any longer and, in effect, committed suicide.

It might be appropriate that we go from horror arising from a father-daughter relationship to horror related to a mother-daughter relationship. And indeed, under any circumstances, the relationship between a female parent and child is fraught with neurosis-breeding pitfalls. For one thing, moms are traditionally responsible for teaching their daughters to be chaste before safely married. This may be difficult to do without in a sense mentally castrating the female child, a process of socialization perhaps symbolized by the title of Germaine Greer's 1970s feminist best-seller *The Female Eunuch*.

Mothers often induce feelings of guilt in their children – male and female -- for both biological and cultural reasons. Biological motherhood and fatherhood are not completely parallel: the latter requires engaging in sexual intercourse while the former requires the enduring of the discomforts of pregnancy, the pain and danger of labor, and the permanent scarring (sometimes distortion) of the body. Even in societies that value gender equality, Mom tends to do more child care than Dad. Thus, there is a sense in which children have a special moral debt to mothers. All-too-easily, this special moral debt can turn into a disabling sense of guilt.

What's more, motherhood is central to most women's identities and with this centrality can come a tendency to tie the child too tightly – in many cases, so tightly that the child is prevented from growing into full adulthood.

In the special case of the mother-daughter relationship, the fact of the two being of the same gender can lead to a kind of "I-thou" confusion that causes such a strong identification between mother and daughter that the love become suffocating and stifling.

The third segment of *Trilogy* draws upon these truths for its horror. When Amelia tells the ugly little fetish doll, "Not even your mother could love you," the statement reflects the overarching importance that a mother's love has had in her life. But her problem, we soon learn, is not that her mother did not love her but that the love is that of a "smother mother." Although Amelia is several years into adulthood, her mother makes her feel guilty for having left the family nest. Although there is no suggestion of sexual incest in this parent-child relationship, there is a kind of dangerous closeness as her mom appears jealous because Amelia has a boyfriend. That mom would be surprised to learn that Amelia has, as she thinks of him, a "fella," shows just how badly this too-close relationship has stunted Amelia's ability to achieve true adulthood. It may be only natural that Amelia feels anger, even an underlying hatred, against the woman who has held onto her so destructively. The horror of the ending is that, freed of the restraints of normal conscience, she will act on the murderous impulses that have long been brewing.

Trilogy of Terror is a cult film that continues to attract new devotees decades after it first aired. That it brilliantly played with, expanded upon, explored, and upended archetypes of female sexuality is a too-often-overlooked basis for the haunted resonance of its horror.

References

Giddins, Gary. "Dark Sky Rising." *The Sun.* Jan. 8, 2008.

Hunter, Dan; Knowles, Jason. "Trilogy of Terror." *The Terror Trap.* http://www.terrortrap.com/trilogyofterror

Kipp, Jeremiah. "DVD Review: *Trilogy of Terror.*" *Slant.* June 20, 2006.

MeTV Staff. "Let's not forget 'Trilogy of Terror' was the scariest TV movie of all time." *MeTV Atlanta.* Oct. 2016.

"Trilogy of Terror (1975)." *Internet Movie Database.* https://www.imdb.com/title/tt0073820/

"Trilogy of Terror." *The Loft Cinema.* https://loftcinema.org/film/trilogy-of-terror/

www.ingramcontent.com/pod-product-compliance
Lightning Source LLC
LaVergne TN
LVHW012026060526
838201LV00061B/4475